Dangerous Music

By: Jack Teeter

PublishAmerica
Baltimore

First printing

At the specific preference of the author, PublishAmerica allowed this work to remain exactly as the author intended, verbatim, without editorial input.

ISBN: 1-4241-0780-6
PUBLISHED BY PUBLISHAMERICA, LLLP
www.publishamerica.com
Baltimore

Printed in the United States of America

Dedication:

To Karen, who lived it with me.

Prologue

Sonny Jacobs woke up in a daze. It took him a minute to realize where he was. "Ungh…I've really been out of it." He adjusted his seat to an upright position.

"Well, good evening, sleepy-head. How're you feeling?" Jenny glanced over at her husband, keeping her attention focused on her driving. "These Nashville people drive like maniacs."

Sonny took a minute, now that he was vertical, to gauge his pain level. He felt a twinge in his neck and some numbness in his shoulders. Unclipping the neurostimulator controller from his belt, he pushed the 'Up' buttons. The unit made beeping sounds for each of his two adjustments. He sensed a surge of current and felt better almost immediately.

"Oh, you know what? I came up with some more of that new song: 'Why Doesn't He Sing'," he told her. "I changed the whatchamacallit? The point of view; I made it a about a musician visiting a church congregation."

"Umm…" Jenny was distracted, thinking about something else. "So, they just embed the power supply under your shoulder blade, right, and attach it to the lead wire implanted in your neck?"

Sonny tried to catch up with her question; apparently she wasn't interested in his new song lyric. "Right…that way everything is internal. It will be a relief, after carrying this around for two weeks." He re-attached the temporary external controller and power supply to the belt on his jeans. "The implanted power pack should last about five years, like Dr. Kinkaid told us. You know all this stuff…it was on that 'Pain Management' tape the manufacturer sent us. What are you asking?"

They were on Interstate 40, about a mile from the Highway 440 exit, at a little before 8:00 PM, Sunday evening. Tomorrow Sonny had a day-surgery appointment at Vanderbilt Medical Center. Today had been clear and warm in Oak Ridge; it was clouding up in Nashville, rain in the forecast. "I hope it doesn't get cold," Jenny observed. "They get more snow here than we do at home."

"Jen?"

She didn't look at him; traffic was heavy as they neared the congested junction. "This construction's almost as bad as Knoxville."

"Earth to Jen…"

She didn't answer until they'd cleared the interchange, cruising again. "I'm just nervous, okay? This whole idea scares me."

Sonny turned his shoulders to face her; the neck-brace he was wearing made the movement awkward. "What scares you, Babe? Are you worried about this second surgery? They don't even have to wake me up for this one; I get to sleep right through it."

She wiped at her eyes with her fingers, not answering.

"Let's stop at Chili's," Sonny suggested. Whatever was bothering her would take some time to resolve. "We can settle in and talk a while. Maybe order some nachos."

"I'd rather just go on to the motel."

Sonny turned back toward the windshield. "Sure, that's fine."

****

They tossed their bags and coats on the extra bed in the motel room. Jenny sat in one of the upholstered straight-backed chairs next to a tiny circular table, Sonny was on the edge of the bed. He gestured at the cooler they'd brought with them. "You want a Pepsi?"

"No, thanks."

He reached to take her hand. "Come on. Whatever it is you're worried about, we'll face it together. Tell me."

She squeezed his hand, and then let it go, leaning back in her chair. "You remember the way those pain medicines affected you? How you had all those bad dreams and things?"

Sonny smiled, relieved to at least know the subject of their conversation. "Sure, that was really bad, but it's been quite a while since…"

She waved her hand, telling him to let her finish. "Sonny, I think the pain, over the last two years, has taken a toll."

Sonny *looked* fine; his erect posture, gray-flecked buzz haircut, and ruddy complexion declared his profession, high school coach. But for two years now he had been on disability from Oak Ridge Senior High, diagnosed with persistent, chronic pain in his neck and shoulders.

She hurried on before he could interrupt. "We've talked before about this, I know. Stopping the medication did stop the bad dreams and paranoia, that's good. But the other things…not remembering why you come into a room, stumbling over words, forgetting people's names…those things aren't getting any better."

Sonny shrugged, wanting to make light of it. "Hey, I'm getting older, Jen. Most of the kids at school would say fifty-two is ancient."

"That's not the point!" she snapped.

"Jenny…" He lifted his hands. "I get it! And I agree. I do struggle sometimes. But it's going to get better. That's what so great about the neuro…neurostimulator system. It stops the pain."

She shook her head. "It *masks* the pain, Sonny. The pulse from the lead wire just overrides the message being sent to your brain. No one, none of the doctors, have said that it will stop the deterioration. They say alleviating the pain will improve your quality of life, but they can't make any promises about the effect the pain has on you."

Sonny leaned forward. "I'm not exactly drooling when I go out in public, am I?"

"Don't you *dare* throw my words back in my face!" she cried out, standing up, glaring at him. "I'm worried. And you should be, too!"

He leaned back so that he could look up at her, regretting what he'd said. "Sorry, but I still don't get it. None of this is new…what is it you're worried about?"

She took a deep breath. "Okay, even if the doctors can't guarantee that blocking the pain will help with the memory loss and other things; that's alright with me. I can see that the device makes a wonderful difference for you."

"So, you agree? The stimulator's a good thing, right?"

"Of course."

"And you're not worried about the surgery?"

"Nope."

He leaned forward again. "Come on. But…"

She turned and walked toward the door. She circled around, pacing in the small space at the foot of the bed. "Alright, back to my original point about the medicines, how they affected you. Sonny, you know what's as bad, or maybe worse, than those meds?"

He didn't answer.

"Your music…"

He laughed uncomfortably. "My music?"

She stopped her pacing, glaring down at him. "That's why I'm worried. Tomorrow the doctors are going to make the stimulator permanent. Tomorrow you'll have the ability to hurt yourself whenever you want to!"

Sonny didn't say anything for a long time.

She touched his face; then leaned down to open the cooler. "I'm ready for a drink, now. You want one?"

"Sure."

He sipped his Coke, trying to make sense out of what she had said. Obviously, Jenny was worried about him 'upping the amps' when he played his music.

Quite by accident one evening last week, when he was playing his guitar to take his mind off the pain, he had set the amperage on his neurostimulator device too high—way too high. The current was supposed to mask pain in his neck and shoulders. Instead, he felt a surge all the way out to his fingertips. He recalled that evening:

"What's it gonna take?" Sonny complained aloud. Despite the higher setting, he could barely move his fingers on the guitar frets for

the pain in his shoulders. Angry, he reached over and held his thumb and index finger against the 'Up' controls, watching the read-out:

3.8—still not enough.

4.2—come on!

4.5—a little more...

The tingling was all the way out to his fingertips now, his elbows felt like he had bumped both his funny bones.

Now, he thought, repositioning the guitar on his knee, give it a few minutes to settle down. He worked the 'D'-chord intro to his song.

"Whoa!" Sonny exclaimed.

He tried the chord progression again.

"What the..." he muttered, his fingers still tingling.

Something was happening...

'D', then 'G', back to 'D', then an 'A'...He closed his eyes, playing through it again. He reached his right hand to his mouth and put the pick between his teeth, then tried the progression again, this time using his thumb and first two fingers to do the strumming.

He spit the pick out on the floor. "Wow!"

Okay, all the way through, but this time with the words:

He said he didn't owe anything to anyone
Didn't have to answer for anything he had done...

The timing...and the rhythm...

And the secrets he thought he was keepin'
seems like everybody knows...

The timing...and the rhythm...and the music! Something was definitely happening! The song Sonny was playing was the song he had imagined when he first wrote it. The chords fit. The transitions were smooth. He was making music, really good music! He played and sang the song—the chorus and the other verses, too—over and over. This was wonderful!

Sonny understood his wife's concern…but the trade off—some funny-bone pain for making wonderful music—was worth it a hundred times over!

"Jen, it's only a temp…temporary pain. And the music is really good!"

She moved to sit on the edge of the bed, next to him. "You still don't get it…Sonny, after your music, when you turn the device back down, and you think you're back to normal?"

He nodded, studying her face.

"You're not! Sonny, after you play, it's awful. You can hardly remember your name."

She absently unscrewed the top of her drink bottle; then set it on the table. "The other day, you said you'd get the clothes out of the dryer when I was on the phone. But you were playing pool when I came down; you'd forgotten all about the laundry.

"And Doug Henson, your best buddy and your catcher when you pitched for the Carson-Newman Eagles…"

"What about Doug?"

"Last night, after you sang for our friends, to see if they could tell the difference in your playing; you couldn't even remember Doug's name when you got done."

"They loved my playing, Jenny, and I *know* who Doug is…" Sonny muttered.

"I loved your playing, too Sonny. That's not the point. What about *later* last night?"

Sonny dropped his eyes. "You mean the extra pain pills? I couldn't get to sleep."

Jenny reached to take his chin in her hand. "I'm not criticizing you, Sonny. I know you were hurting. That's the point. You had to take extra pills, just to get to sleep last night. And you didn't wake up until after ten this morning."

"Truth is, I've been pretty much out of it all day," Sonny admitted, touching her hand as she released his chin. "I don't even remember packing for this trip."

"You didn't, I packed your bag."

He raised his eyebrows but didn't comment.

"Earlier, when you woke up to tell me about your new song; that was the first time you've been really alert all day. You've been a zombie since right after you stopped playing last night."

Sonny jumped up off the bed! "What did you call me!" he yelled. "Did you just call me a zombie?"

Jenny glared at him; she got up from the bed herself. "Calm down," she said, her voice cold and controlled. "Back off!"

"Dang!" Sonny slammed the flat of his hand on the table, jolting the hotel's empty glass coffeepot onto the floor.

They both stared down at the broken container. Jenny raised her eyes to his, sighing heavily.

"What in the world am I doing…" Sonny's eyes filled with tears. "What's happening to me, Jenny?"

He reached down to retrieve the broken glass, carefully placing the pieces into the trash container near the dresser, and then looked at his wife. "I'm sorry."

"I know you are," she said, reaching for him.

She held him for a few moments. Sonny didn't try to pull away; he collapsed into her arms, needing her comfort. "You know I'd never say those things to hurt you, don't you?" she said.

"It's okay, Jenny. I know that's not the way you meant it."

After another long embrace she stiffened, straightening her posture. She sat back down on the bed, looking up at him. She had to get it all out, had to tell him how she felt. "Sonny?"

He stared at her, reading her eyes. "Yeah?"

She didn't let go of his eyes with her gaze; Jenny wanted her husband to understand. "Using the neurostimulator to hurt yourself deliberately, to make music, is dangerous. Your music is dangerous, Sonny!"

Chapter 1

The Second Avenue exit is the passage to downtown Nashville from Interstate 40. Jenny stayed on the one-way street, straight through the bustling Broadway intersection.

Even fierce mid-March winds couldn't keep visitors away from the Capital of Country Music. To hundreds of out-of-town tourists from up north, the current temperature of 46 degrees was a heat wave. Broad spans of the sidewalk on both sides of the street were in shade, but dazzling marquee lights brightened the gaps where sunlight couldn't reach. There were gaudy T-shirts featuring pictures of country artists, wide-brimmed feathers-in-the-headband cowboy hats, and genuine leather boots available for purchase! And music was blaring from every doorway.

At the far north end, where Second intersected with Church Street, Jenny found a Central Parking lot, the kind with the honor-system fee machines. "Look around," she told Sonny, "help me remember where we're parked."

Straight ahead, on Union Street, was the Davidson County Courthouse; to the east, across a busy highway, they could see the grandstands of the Coliseum, where the pro football Titans played.

Sonny retrieved his imitation-leather guitar case from the trunk. After feeding $5.00 to the auto-pay meter, they crossed Church Street. He was tempted to stop for hot wings and a gape at the waitresses in the crowded Hooters on their left, but Jenny tugged his arm, heading them up Church toward the neon 'Printers Alley' arch that spanned the street.

A construction crew had left detour signs, blocking pedestrian traffic away from a deep muddy hole in the sidewalk. They walked left, up Third, turning their backs to the cold breeze. Sonny beeped twice, upping his amperage; compensating for the increased stiffness in his shoulders caused by their walking. The next cross street was Commerce. Demos' Steak & Spaghetti House customers were waiting in line; huddled against the red brick wall, out of the wind. Ahead on Broadway, 'Red Iguana' in huge ugly red letters covered the wall for half a block. Next door, in smaller black letters, was the sign for Wanda's Karaoke Bar.

They turned right on Broadway, joining the crowd, ignoring the 'Don't Walk' crossing sign at Fourth Avenue, headed toward their destination, the corner of Broadway and Fifth.

"I'm trying to take all this in," Sonny remarked, looking across the way where a huge awning marked the Earnest Tubb Record Shop, next to a place called Wolfy's. "Last time we were here, I was too nervous to soak up any of the at…atmosphere."

They had to stop for a surge of patrons coming out of a place called Second Fiddle. A chunky woman in a flowery short-sleeved western shirt noticed Sonny's guitar case. "Are you somebody famous?" She studied the tall thin man's appearance: burgundy ball cap with interlocking 'O R', ordinary black nylon jacket, straight-legged jeans, worn running shoes, and the dilapidated guitar case.

"Nah, I'm nobody…" Sonny chuckled.

"What was I thinking?" the woman asked her companion as they hurried away to the next attraction.

As the crowd spread out, going in all directions, Jenny could make out the sign for Legends Corner, featuring 'Country Music Souvenirs, Fine Food, and Live Entertainment'. "I don't see Tootsies…"

"Oh, wait!" Sonny grasped her arm. "Here it is!"

Without realizing it, they were stopped right in front of the garish, shamelessly-purple entrance to Tootsies Orchid Lounge. In the display case to the right of the doorway hung three framed, autographed pictures: Willie Nelson, Terri Clark and a bearded guy neither of them recognized. On the other side Chris Kristofferson, Faron Young and Ronnie McDowell were featured. In the doorway itself, on the glass partition, was a tattered flier. 'Introducing John Stone and his latest hit Shame On Me'. The entryway screamed out 'Honky Tonk'! Just what the tourists were looking for—the place was jammed.

****

An extraordinarily-long blond braid trailed out the back of the John Deere cap of the singer on the bandstand, just inside. His James Taylor solo left the rhythm guitar and bass player nodding their heads in time to the music, eyeing the couple squeezing through the half-open entry door. The man lugging the guitar case was unremarkable, but the woman with him was striking, a dazzling long-legged redhead in tight jeans!

The barstooled greeter grabbed Jenny's arm as they came in. "Where y'all from?" He smiled and handed Sonny a gaudy purple flyer. They could barely make out his question above the noise of the crowd. Sound reverberated off the bare-brick walls and cracked concrete floor; people were yelling, making flamboyant gestures with their beer bottles; having a good time. The singer's rendition of "Carolina On My Mind" sounded as good as JT himself.

Sonny glanced at the flyer—everything you could possibly want to know about World Famous Tootsies Orchid Lounge—then stuffed it into his back pocket. "Oak Ridge!" he yelled his answer to the greeter's question, possessively circling his arm around Jenny's waist.

"Well, y'all come on in!" the greeter hollered, flashing a bright smile at Jenny. The raw-boned young man couldn't have been any more cordial had Sonny announced they were from Kalamazoo. "Getcha a drink on your way through," he advised, moving his chin toward the bar to make sure he was understood above the commotion, "the barmaid may never find ya!"

Sonny hoisted his guitar case up under his arm as they pushed ahead. He ordered two Bud Lights and they worked their way to an open barstool. High, round tables were scattered around the long narrow room. Clusters of cups, bottles, and crumpled bags of chips covered every surface, each table shared by more patrons than fit on the two or three stools allotted.

The space behind the bar was covered with autographed photos; most were framed, but some were just tacked to the aged curling wallpaper. A glass case displaying stacks of authentic Tootsies T-shirts and caps was unopened; the crowd was more interested in partying than purchasing souvenirs.

Jenny boosted up onto the stool, taking a gulp of her beer and winking across the table at two young guys in brand new cowboy hats; the two men had turned their attention away from the bandstand as she took off her jacket. Sonny wedged his guitar into a space under the table and rested one hand on the back of his wife's barstool.

The band transitioned into "Margaritaville," recapturing the young men's attention. They raised their bottles, saluting the couple and the familiar good times anthem.

From a short half-flight of stairs behind them, an attractive blonde barmaid worked her way toward them, gesturing at Sonny's guitar case. "Y'all better get a move on," she yelled into Jenny's ear, pointing back toward the stairs, "John's already said 'Last Call'!"

The couple just looked at her.

"Billy saw you come in." The barmaid absently waved a hand at the greeter, still on his stool near the entry door. "He figured you were running late. He sent Carley up to tell me."

Her explanation still didn't register; they continued to gawk at her. The intensity in the slender blonde's eyes urged them to hurry, but what on earth was she talking about?

She had had enough dilly-dallying. "Get your gear and come on!" she commanded, nodding at Sonny's guitar case. She turned to go, then remembered to ask, "What's y'all's name? So I can introduce you."

"Jacobs…" Sonny started to tell the pretty young woman, but she was already on her way up the stairs before he could finish.

"Hey, come back here!" he hollered belligerently, then thought better of getting upset. He shook his head and mumbled after her into empty space. "Sonny Jacobs."

He shrugged and looked at his wife. "I thought 'open mic' didn't start until six?" Jenny raised her palms in front of her chest. "That's what they told me…"

"What?" He couldn't make out what she said. He reached down for his case.

"Never mind." She shook her head, giving up on being heard. The crowd was singing along to a line of the Buffett song.

I blew out my flip-flop, stepped on a pop top.

She pulled Sonny's arm, grabbing up their coats. "Let's get a move on!"

****

Sonny followed his wife up the five concrete steps to the upper level of the Honky Tonk. Two guitar players were just finishing Brooks & Dunn's "How Long Gone" on the stage at the far end of the room.

The building's old brick walls were great soundproofing. Unless you were standing on the stairs, you couldn't tell there were two separate lounges, two separate sound stages. The upper level wasn't quite as packed as downstairs; the customers clapped and hooted when the kids on stage finished their song, showing their approval.

"Thanks guys," a tall thick-waisted man told them from a sound console to the left of the bandstand, "we'll be in touch." He turned and looked toward the rear stairs. Every eye followed his; Sonny and Jenny felt like they'd just yelled 'FIRE!' in the crowded room.

"Ladies and gentlemen…" It was the barmaid that had fetched them, speaking into one of the on-stage microphones. "We've got one more audition, a couple. They call themselves 'Jacob'. The crowd finished eyeing them, and then turned back toward the stage.

"They'll be with us here in a minute, but let's hear it one more time for Tim and Todd," the barmaid exhorted, "The UpSiders!" The crowd offered another supportive round of applause then started random conversations, ignoring the next artists as they made their way toward the stage.

"'A couple'…she thinks I'm a singer, too!" Jenny giggled to Sonny as they worked their way forward. She jabbed her husband in the ribs.

****

"What'll it be, little lady?" The man at the console addressed Jenny, "Are we talking Bonnie Raitt or Reba?"

"Oh, no…" Jenny laughed. "It's not like that."

"Okay, a duo then." John turned his attention to Sonny. "An acoustic, huh?" Gesturing at the guitar case, he reached behind him, pulling a miniature wireless microphone from a box of techie gizmos.

Sonny looked nervously around the room, absently tugging at the bill of his Oak Ridge ball cap, deciding to leave it on while he performed. His stress level elevated at the thought of actually performing; he needed to get to the controller in his pocket.

Before he could answer, Jenny spoke for him, "Sorry, John, is it?"

The man nodded, offering his hand. "John Tyler. I'm the talent coordinator here." He frowned. "What are we sorry about?"

"My husband's the singer," she told him, taking Sonny's elbow. "I'm just a groupie."

John Tyler smiled at the redhead. *Too bad*, he thought to himself, then, *what the heck; give the old guy a shot.*

It had already been a good session, with a little practice Tim and Todd would be dead ringers for Brooks & Dunn. He turned his smile on Sonny, handing him the electronic pickup. "Just clip it on, Jacob, and we'll do a sound check." He turned to his console, making adjustments.

Sonny didn't bother to correct the man; it didn't really matter what they called him. He spotted a bench at the side of the stage. He opened his case over there, and sat down, fastening on his shoulder strap, and strumming a 'C' chord to check his tuning. Without turning around, he slipped the neurostimulator control from the pocket of his shirt and held it over the power pack beneath his collarbone, ratcheting the amperage up eight counts.

Within seconds he felt the surge in his neck and shoulders and down into his arms. He pushed the 'Up' buttons twice more, feeling the current all the way to his fingertips; then slipped the device back into his pocket.

He clipped the electronic pickup to the soundboard of his guitar.

"Ready when you are," he called out to the man at the console. He stepped up to the microphone on the right—the one Todd had been using—and strummed a 'C' chord, getting a feel for the amplified resonance.

The crowd, used to the mechanics of sound checks, ignored Sonny, talking animatedly about the other talent they had seen that afternoon.

The barmaid called to Jenny, "Over here…" She patted the seat of the barstool next to her.

"Hey, do I recognize your voice?" Jenny asked. "Are you the woman I talked with on the phone?"

"I'm Susan," the young woman answered. "I get a lot of calls. I manage the place." She watched the redhead's expression change; her green eyes were amused at someone so young being in charge. "Really," the woman assured her, "I do."

"Oh my goodness, I didn't mean…"

"Happens all the time…" Susan grinned. "Don't give it a second thought."

****

Sonny was ready.

Not a single head turned his way as he played the opening 'Am'-'Em'-'D' chord progression to "Angel With The Light In His Eyes." He let his fingers stretch out, beginning to tell their story. He began to draw a dark night with his strings, as if he were painting on a canvas. His voice and fingers told the story of a weary man, tired from a long day, hurrying to beat the storm home.

A woman in the front row shushed her husband and his friend. Another man set his drink down, caught up in the minor-chord rhythm.

I pulled in the drive, under stormy skies
I was tired and the hour was late…

Sonny's voice was engaging, willing them to listen. Another couple quieted, wondering…His playing fashioned the garden for them. And, quite suddenly, he made the vision of an angel appear. The few people who were listening could see a light, shining brightly from the angel's eyes.

When I saw the angel with the light in his eyes
Standing by my garden gate...

More and more groups stopped their conversations, tuning in. A man whispered to his wife, trying to catch up with the story; she didn't look away to answer.

By the time his fingers and voice had allowed the audience to look with the angel, into the tired traveler's first bedroom, almost everyone was still.

The light shined first on my child as he slept
and I was able to see his dreams
I saw the loves in his heart and the secrets he kept
but none of them included me

Sonny started the chorus.

Then my heart turned cold as I realized
The light was shining on me...

Now almost everyone was paying attention, watching the man with the acoustic guitar, looking right through the hole that the angel's light had burned into his heart. Sonny's song enthralled them; they wanted to look into the next room though the angel's eyes, wanted to gaze over Sonny's shoulder at his grandfather's bible.

The light shined last on a dusty shelf
on a book that was old and worn
My grandfather's bible sat all by itself
as I read it my heart grew warm

When the haunting song ended, Sonny pushed his ball cap back on his forehead, an old coaching habit—he did that whenever there was a break in the action of a game. He looked out at his audience, waiting for their reaction. A man in the back, the one who had set his drink aside earlier, began to clap. His hands made a slow steady beat, louder with each clap, acknowledging Sonny's performance. Soon, everyone in the room was caught up in that slow, steady, clapping beat.

"My God, what a song…" a woman said.

"I could see the garden, the angel, everything…" a man told his wife.

"Thank you," Sonny softly spoke into the microphone, flashing a bright smile.

No one but Jenny could tell how much the song had taken out of him. His face was sweating and his body was rigid, but to his audience that was just the storyteller's style. His intense demeanor made his performance all the more personal, made his yarn all the more believable.

Susan let the applause run its course; then approached Sonny's microphone. "How about another song?" she prompted.

Sonny tugged his cap back into place—back to business. The crowd quieted; they weren't going to miss a single note this time, not a word of his next story would get by them.

"Jacob…" the blonde announced again, and moved aside.

Sonny closed his eyes for a moment, gathering his energy; then began picking the up-tempo chord intro to his song about an old Rocker.

We heard he didn't pick much any more
Just now and then a lick or two, or a couple of minor chords

When he got to the chorus, the audience—his friends now—clapped along with the heavy beat.

But they knew he could make it wail
They knew, if he let her rip, that he could drive that nail…

When the applause died down after this second song, John Tyler stood up. He made a point of looking at his watch. "Auditions are over for this evening," he announced. There were a few murmurs from the crowd. He turned and addressed Sonny, his voice loud enough for the audience to listen in, "You can come back and do a couple songs during 'open mic', can't you?"

Sonny nodded, making his way to the bench behind him. He had to get the amperage turned down—he was exhausted!

He hurried with his adjustments. As the current lessened, he felt the tension ebb away. Jenny rushed to his side, stepping in front of him to hide his movements as best she could. "I thought *that* was 'open mic'?" Sonny asked her.

"Guess not…" That's all she was able to get out before they were crowded with admirers.

****

The barmaid / manager announced a twenty-minute break, encouraging the crowd to 'Stop and give a listen to our house band downstairs, everyone! Gerry, the guy with the long braid, does a great James Taylor. Oh, and don't forget to check out our T-shirts and caps, one of the barmaids can fix you right up!'

Four couples crowded around Sonny. He pushed his ball cap back on his head and reached out to greet the closest person, offering his hand from where he was sitting. Jenny nudged his elbow, and then winked when he looked at her, prompting him to stand. He took the hint.

"Where y'all from?" he asked, struggling to his feet.

A lanky fellow pulled at the front of his sweatshirt. "Wisconsin! Like the shirt says. We're from Janesville, south of Madison, right on the border. Down here to see the sights in Nashville."

"We loved your singing!" His wife joined the conversation, a portly woman with an ill-fitting straw hat. "I was telling Herb, last thing I thought we'd hear in a place like this was an angel song. It was a wonderful song, real moving!"

"Well, thanks!" Sonny said. It was easy to be enthusiastic after the euphoria of his performance. "Glad you folks liked it! What do you do, up in Wisconsin?"

"You mean for a living? Or what kind of shows do we have up there?"

And so it went…

Jenny joined in the conversations—the starry-eyed wife—spelling her husband as his adrenalin wore off and fatigue set in. Sonny had to use the controller once; despite how it might appear, his increasing pain level left him no choice. The woman they were talking to wasn't forward enough to comment, but the question was on her face. Sonny chose to ignore the look, steering her in another direction. "What kind of music do *you* generally listen to? Country, I'd guess, you being from Tulsa."

As they were talking, Susan began lugging a barstool up onto the stage, placing it near one of the mic stands. She went to get another. Apparently 'open mic' was a sit-down affair. Jenny smiled at the thought; that would be easier on Sonny.

"We'd better take advantage of our break time…Honey," she said, interrupting his conversation with one last admiring couple. Sonny was signing a Tootsies T-shirt that the husband had hustled down to purchase. Jenny hesitated before calling her husband 'Honey'. Was he going to go by his new stage name, 'Jacob'? Or would he go back to being 'Sonny'?

John Tyler motioned for Sonny to come by the console area. He lifted a guitar from a stand behind him. "Great job, Buddy!" he said.

There was no 'y'all' in his voice; 'Buddy' was more Midwestern. John noticed their reaction. He smiled. "Trying to figure out my accent, huh? I'm a Chicago boy, born and bred. The customers expect me to lay on the southern twang…

"Anyways," he continued, holding out the guitar to Sonny, "…a little reward for pleasing the customers. You can borrow this when you do your 'open mic' set. It'll make the intro to that old Rocker song stronger."

Sonny hesitated.

"Go on, pick a few chords; see how a real guitar feels."

"That's a Strato…Stratocaster," Sonny said. "I…"

John insisted, handing it to him. "Go plug it in."

Sonny walked over to one of the barstools, locating a jack plug, lying on the floor. The Stratocaster didn't even buzz when he plugged it in. He strummed the chords for "House Of The Rising Sun." The Fender guitar felt wonderful in his hands. The frets were low and smooth. Moving across the strings didn't sting his fingertips; he could get used to this!

John was looking at him, his head cocked to one side, like he'd heard something out-of-place in Sonny's playing.

Then it hit Sonny: even for the familiar chord progression, his playing was sluggish, discordant. Of course! He hadn't turned up his stimulator. Hurriedly, he pulled the amplifier plug.

"Hey!" a voice yelled from the back of the room. Two men had come up from the lower level; they were munching popcorn, guzzling their beers. "You started it, Pardner," the larger of the two yelled, "keep goin'! I like that song."

With the guitar plug still in his hand, Sonny glanced at John. John scowled and nodded his head toward the rear of the room. 'A customer,' the gesture said, 'play!'

Jenny was watching. She could tell the situation was escalating Sonny's stress level. *Don't do it!* She pleaded within herself, willing her husband to maintain his composure. *Don't get angry!*

Sonny saw his wife's reaction out of the corner of his eye. Just in time, he reined in his anger. She saw him take a deep breath and let it out slowly.

He would comply with the customer's request, but first he had to get the current of his stimulator going. He stepped down from the stool, turning his back as he pulled the controller from his pocket and hurriedly hiked up the amperage, eight notches. He didn't take time to see how it felt—whether the setting was too weak or too strong—he had to play!

The setting wasn't perfect, a little weak; it took all of Sonny's self-control to ignore the throbbing in his neck. He eased back up onto the barstool, tugged again at his ball cap and plugged the jack back in, and then leaned into the microphone.

There is a house in New Orleans
They call the Rising Sun…

He finished the song. John's encouraging grin told him that he'd played it well. The guys in the back had left before he finished. There was a smattering of polite applause from a few people still at tables. Sonny unplugged the Stratocaster.

"Thanks," he said, returning the instrument to its owner, "that was really great!"

"Customer's always right," John said, pointing his thumb over his shoulder toward the back of the room. "Any time you step up to that mic, people want to hear you play, even if we're on break!"

Sonny looked out at the clusters of people, eating their chips, sipping their drinks. "The guy that yelled," Sonny observed, "him and his buddy left before I even finished."

"Hey, that's the entertainment business for ya."

Jenny had hurried to retrieve Sonny's guitar from the rear bench. She could almost see his shoulders jumping in response to the high amperage. He needed to get it turned back down—right now! She handed him the case. "We'd better take advantage of our break."

To John she said, "That fancy guitar sounded great! We'll be back for 'open mic'…"

John was distracted; putting the Fender guitar back in its place, ready to take a break himself. "No hurry," he muttered; his back to them.

He turned his head, deciding maybe his tone was a little too terse. "There'll be a few locals. They usually bring their own crowd. We'll let some of them go ahead of you guys."

"We'll be back after a while," Sonny said. It took every ounce of energy he could muster not to moan as he spoke. "Thanks for everything."

"You bet," John replied as they left.

He had noticed Sonny's furtive movements before playing. *No telling what antics people go through to get ready to perform,* he'd thought at the time. The man had turned his back and pulled something from his shirt pocket. He didn't take a drink or inhale, as John had seen others do, rather, he held—whatever it was—to his chest.

Strange guy, John told himself, *pretty good songwriter, though.*

Chapter 2

A tall glass of milk was Sonny's greatest need when they sat down in a booth next to the window in Rippy's Ribs & BBQ, right across the street from Tootsies. He'd stopped to turn down his stimulator as soon as they were out of the talent coordinator's sight. Now he was beeping every couple of minutes, up two, down one, trying to find a comfortable setting.

His milk arrived and he set the controller on the table. "Close enough," he declared.

"Maybe if you eat something," Jenny suggested. "You only had a bowl of soup for lunch." She turned to the waitress. "How's your hamburger steak, Miss?"

The waitress had seen her customer holding what looked like a remote up to his shoulder; it had made a beeping sound. She was mesmerized.

"What does that thing do?" she asked Sonny, pointing at the controller, there on the tabletop. "The way your eyes were jumping, it looked like you were zapping yourself!"

Sonny finished gulping the whole glass of milk before he answered. "That's about right, actually. It's a pain regulator."

She frowned, trying to understand.

"Works pretty good except when I'm tired and hungry…" His voice took an edge. "How about that hamburger steak?"

The waitress continued to gape at him. "Why do you hold it up to your shoulder? Got one of those pacemaker things under there, I bet, right?"

Sonny refused to participate any further in the Q & A session. Jenny could see that he was on the edge, but he struggled to stay calm. "You'll have to excuse me," he said, getting up from the booth, slipping the controller into his pocket on his way to the restroom.

Jenny glared at the waitress, a thin girl, barely 18, probably working part time, after school and weekends. "I'll have the hamburger steak, too." She touched her still-full glass of Coke. "I'm okay on this."

"Yes, Ma'am," the girl huffed. All she did was ask a simple question…what was the big deal? She didn't bother to write anything on her order pad before turning to leave—two hamburger steaks weren't that hard to remember.

Sonny did feel better after they started eating. "Jen?"

"Yes?"

"Let's make a deal. I need you to concentrate on how our tryout or whatever this is…concentrate on how we're doing. What we need to do next. Help me with talking to people."

Jenny put her fork down. "And just what do you think I've been doing?"

He grinned. "Worrying about me, worrying how I'm feeling, how bad my pain is. If I'm gonna slip-up—overreact…that's what I think you've been doing. That's not what we need to concentrate on."

He took her hand. "I'll make it, okay? If I spend the next week in bed recuperating, so be it. We've got to stay…on task. See if we can get something positive out of this trip." He let go of her hand. "Agreed?"

She took a drink before answering, "Okay, I agree." Her eyes probably betrayed her words; she couldn't help worrying. But she *would* try! "Eyes on the prize, right, Coach?" She grinned.

Sonny nodded. "Now you're talking, Babe. We'll find a way to get through this. Good job with the…those people, while ago. I hate small talk, but I know that's a part of it. I need to smile and play nice—maybe they'll buy a CD someday."

The high school girl came back around, bringing their orders. "Sorry if I was short with you, young lady." Sonny offered her a huge smile. "Sometimes this gizmo…" He pointed his fork at his shoulder blade. "…acts up a little. That makes me cranky."

The girl frowned again.

"Do you forgive me?" her customer asked.

She shrugged, then remembered to smile, there was a tip riding on her attitude. "Sure, no problem, Sir." She even showed the snippy lady her happy face. "Anything else I can get y'all?"

When neither answered, she placed their bill on the table. "I'll check on y'all again in a few minutes."

"Despite the confusion—I guess since that wasn't 'open mic' it was some sort of audition—it went really well, didn't you think?" Jenny asked as the girl left. "After they started paying attention, the crowd really got into it."

"Oh, and I caught your look when that guy in the back made me play 'Rising Sun'." He grinned at her. "That was good, I was about to lose it! You saw me take that deep breath, get myself together, didn't you?"

She nodded.

"See, I'm really trying. I want us to get something out of this trip." He laughed. "I can't believe I had to waste jolting myself a second time for that jerk. He and his pal left before I even finished.

"But hey, playing that Stra…Fender guitar, was wild! I could learn to love an instrument like that. Those things are expensive, though. The mini-transmitter thing he gave me worked fine on my acoustic."

He touched his finger to his temple. "That thing is still clipped onto my guitar. Remind me to give it back to him."

"John seems like a nice guy." Jenny pushed her plate away. "I can't eat another bite. I think we failed his audition, though.

"Did you notice? Susan mentioned that the guy up front sounded like James Taylor. Tim and Todd were doing Brooks & Dunn…

"That's what the crowd wants in a place like Tootsies, something familiar."

"Right…or something *new* that sounds familiar. Remember when that company—the one when I won the contest—they took my song…" Sonny thought a minute. "That same song actually, wasn't it? 'Angel In

The Driveway' as you call it. Anyway, they made it sound like a bunch of other Country songs. You're right, Tootsies is looking for, what's the word? 'Usual', 'ordinary', like medicine?"

"Generic?"

"Yeah, that's it…My songs aren't generic, they paint a picture; you have to pay attention or you'll miss something."

"They loved your songs, Hon!"

Now he pushed his plate away. "I guess I've had enough, too," he said, beeping himself down two clicks, feeling better. "Eating helped a lot, like you said."

Reading her eyes, he hurried to agree with her assessment of the crowd's reaction. "Oh, don't get me wrong, the crowd loved the songs. I think if we can figure out *how*, we can catch a real break! That's what we still need to find out—tonight if we can—is *how*? Now that we know people like our songs, we need to figure out *how* to get someone to buy our music?"

"Ready to get back over there?" Jenny smiled.

Sonny let his shoulders sag, closing his eyes for a minute. "Let me order another small milk, get my stomach good and settled. John said there'd be some others ahead of us."

He gazed around the room, looking for their waitress. "There she is." He signaled to her and ordered his milk. "I thought of something else, just then."

"About others being ahead of us?" she prompted.

"Oh, I remember. Should I sing the same songs again, or try something else? I'd really only planned on doing the 'Driveway' song. Throwing in the Rocker number was already a bonus. What do you think?"

The waitress came back with his milk, jotting the addition on their ticket.

"You can ask John, or I'll ask Susan. We'll see how it goes." Jenny slumped back in the red-plastic booth seat. "I don't mind a little rest myself. There's a lot going on.

"We need a translator," Jenny added. "This whole process has been like visiting a foreign country. I'm not even sure about your name; are you Sonny or Jacob?"

Sonny laughed. "That was bizarre, wasn't it? Maybe we should just let it go. Jacob sounds Biblical. Jacob wrestled with an angel. With the songs I sing, maybe that'll help."

Chapter 3

A full band was playing on the lower level, complete with a drummer and keyboard player. A stunning girl, a white 10-gallon hat atop her long dark hair, was singing. At 6:45 on a Sunday evening, the crowd was more subdued. There was now real food on the tables, hotdogs and pizza slices replacing popcorn and potato chips. The band's version of "Girls Lie Too" sounded just like Terri Clark's original.

Sonny was still taken aback by the transition as they climbed the short staircase to the upper level at Tootsies. There were two complete nightclubs; separate bars, and separate performing platforms. On the upper level, a stocky cowboy was alone with his guitar at one of the on-stage barstools. He was 'Western' from his pointed boots up to his big black cowboy hat. He wore an embroidered pearl-buttoned shirt over stiff jeans with a huge shiny belt buckle.

They would find out later the cowboy's name was Joel Reed, a popular club performer. Joel hadn't made that one big hit record yet, but he had a good following locally. "I'm gonna do 'Gentle On My Mind' for y'all," the cowboy guitar player was saying, "that's usually a crowd pleaser."

There were hoots and hollers from two tables in the corner; the singer had brought some folks along with him. They were a conservative group, in dress shirts and trousers, nursing Styrofoam cups of Coke rather than bottles of beer. "But after a while, I want you to hear a new song I'm working on," Joel told them. "It's a Nashville Arts Council project, a show they're doing later on this spring. They were kind enough to ask me to write some original songs…"

The din of conversation increased; chairs scraped the floor—the singer realized he was talking too much—the crowd was growing impatient. "Well," he said, an urgency coming into his voice, "y'all came for the singin'! Let's get to it. Here's a great Glen Campbell favorite."

It's knowin' that your door is always open and your path is free to walk…

Sonny walked over to the far corner of the bar and gestured toward the bartender, silently asking permission to stow his guitar case. When she nodded, he held up two fingers and mouthed "Bud Light." He and Jenny carried their drinks to a table near the front.

Maybe the singing cowboy wasn't so young after all. Now that they were closer, he looked to be in his mid-30s, slim and lithe, but there were lines in the sharp angles of his face. "Sounds just like Glen Campbell." Jenny observed, her mouth close to her husband's ear. Sonny didn't think she meant it as a compliment.

The Arts Council song wasn't a crowd pleaser. After the first verse, some of the audience decided that their interrupted conversations could continue. Joel pressed ahead. His guitar work was good, but the lyrics were jumbled. Even his entourage wasn't very enthusiastic with their applause. He rushed into "Wichita Lineman" to get his feet back under him and the crowd back on his side.

Jenny looked around for Susan. John Tyler was in his spot, manning the sound console; a blue-jeaned brunette barmaid was working her away around the tables. But Susan was nowhere to be seen. Maybe no introductions were needed for 'open mic'.

Validating Jenny's assumption, Joel spoke up after finishing his song, "Emma, I see you over there, Emma."

A skinny woman, with spiked black hair and pasty Gothic makeup, stood and waved to acknowledge him. Her entourage, at several tables in the opposite corner, was large and boisterous; they banged their beer bottles on the tabletops and clapped their support as she made her way forward.

"Emma Emerson, folks!" Joel said. "Emma Emerson from Nashville's own KTMQ."

The woman advanced to chants of "Em-ma! Em-ma!" She hugged Joel's neck when she reached the stage and then stepped back as if to appraise his appearance. "This cowboy has got it going on…" She breathed into the microphone.

"Great job, Joel…Joel's new album, 'Falling In Place', has been getting some heavy air time on KTMQ, on our After-Midnight Country Hour." She waved over to her support corner. "You *have* been listening, haven't you, Dahlings…" she vamped. They whooped their response.

"What's Nashville's best Alternative Rock DJ got for us this evenin', Emma?" Joel asked. "Don't tell us you're going Country!"

The woman ran her hands along the length of her slinky black dress. "Just here to see and be seen," she purred. Her followers barked again.

"Play nice and take your seat, baby," she told Joel. "Mommy has a nice surprise for everyone." She grabbed the microphone from its stand and nodded over at John. "Let's do it, Mr. Soundman!"

An inharmonious jumble of noise, with a sub-woofer-shaking bass line, screamed out over the amplifiers at the front of the stage and from the speakers mounted at the rear of the room. Emma lurched about, gyrating her hips and shaking her head to the heavy bass notes. When the Vamp began to wail and moan—her lyrics were as addled as her movements—no one was trying to understand, they were just taking it all in!

Sonny had to pull off his cap to hide his face. Jenny got caught up in the moment and joined in, clapping along with the dog-pound in Emma's corner. Only a few white-shirt-and-tie customers from Joel's group didn't join the weird cacophony; everyone else in the audience was clapping loudly and shouting her name. "Em-ma! Em-ma!"

The song lasted for what seemed like half an hour. Sonny, no longer trying to contain his amusement, caught John's eye. The soundman rolled his eyes and shook his head.

Finally the—whatever it was—came to an end. Emma raised her arms over her head, causing her tight dress to ride up immodestly, in response to the crowd's robust support. When they finally settled down, she pulled at the hem of her dress and put the microphone back on its stand. "Thanks, Dahlings…" she breathed again, "it's been divine."

She promptly left the stage.

"Oh my God," Jenny whispered to Sonny. "I hope you're not following *that*!"

****

Joel Reed saved them. He walked back up to the bandstand, retrieving his guitar from where he'd left it on the bench Sonny had used earlier. He approached the microphone and waved toward the stairway at the rear of the long room. As Emma Emerson and her followers made a rowdy exodus in the other direction, the Terri Clark look-alike from the downstairs band made her way forward.

The crowd, now appreciably smaller, offered thin applause as Joel announced, "Ladies and Gentlemen, star of her own new group, Country Connections, direct from right downstairs here in Tootsies Orchid Lounge, Miss Toni Clarkson!"

Toni's megawatt smile and willowy cowgirl-clad figure made it easy for the crowd to watch her as she approached the stage. "Come on up, Toni," Joel encouraged.

She gave him the obligatory hug and walked to the other microphone to give the crowd an energetic greeting. "Howdy everybody! How is everyone this fine Sunday evenin'?

"I heard some commotion up here and figured I'd better come up here and remind John." She waved toward the sound console. "That this here is a *Country Bar*!"

Joel and the crowd clapped their agreement. "So I came up here to sing y'all some *Country* music!" Toni proclaimed.

She and Joel had obviously worked this through in advance. He played an intro and she gave a first-rate rendition of "Better Things To

Do." Joel played and sang backup to a couple more Terri Clark songs. Some of the audience from the lower level had made their way upstairs, swelling the room to nearly half-full. The crowd—entertained as they expected to be—showed their appreciation with genuine applause at the end of each song.

"Toni and I are gonna do a couple du-ets after we take a little break," Joel announced when they'd finished "Everytime I Cry." He hopped down off his barstool and nodded toward the sound console. "John, over there, was tellin' me, the folks at Tootsies heard a brand new talent earlier this afternoon."

Jenny looked at Sonny. He stood and leaned sideways, half concealed by the tall table, and reached into his pocket. He pointed the controller and made his adjustments, taking his time, waiting for it to feel right, before straightening back up.

In the mean time, Joel was continuing with Sonny's introduction. "A fella just wandered in off the street with his guitar and blew everyone's socks off! Isn't that right, John?"

John stood up; he nodded and waved at Joel—then motioned to Sonny.

"Song about an angel," the cowboy told Toni, "seems to me that's just the right kinda song for a Sunday evenin'."

Toni nodded her agreement, sliding down off her stool. "This new talent got a name, Joel?"

Joel looked again at John. "Jacob? Isn't that right?"

John nodded again as Sonny worked his way toward him. "So," Joel said, "without further ado…Ladies and Gentlemen: Jacob." He and the girl singer left the stage, shaking Sonny's hand as they moved toward Joel's corner of tables.

The crowd made no response to Joel's introduction—reserving judgment, Jenny supposed. She watched with everyone else as John handed Sonny the Stratocaster and he made his way to the closest microphone. After plugging the guitar in, he gave a tug to his ball cap and slid up on the barstool. He fingered a long, slow 'C'-chord and leaned forward into the microphone.

Lord, we sure could use a miracle today

The words weren't just the opening line to a song; Sonny delivered the lyric as if it were a prayer.

Only a few the people in Joel's corner were making any noise, greeting their stars. Upon hearing the on-stage performer's one-line prayer, they immediately turned quiet.

With the next line of his song, Sonny turned from preacher to storyteller.

I wasn't list'ning for angels singing when I woke up today
And I stopped looking for miracles somewhere along the way…

The crowd gave their attention to the guy in the ball cap, wanting to help him find his angel. Sonny's song changed tempo, taking on a mystical quality with the next verse. A voice was speaking to him in the story, explaining where to look for his angel.

A voice said: Look into the mirror and tell me what you see.
Look beyond your own reflection, where only eyes of faith can see…

But the man in Sonny's song didn't understand. How could he see angels if his heart didn't believe?

But when I look in the mirror, Lord, my reflection is all I see
I can't see angels, when my heart does not believe…

This was Sunday night church! Whether the listeners were from Tupelo or the Twin Cities, they listened. How could they help him believe? Sonny's guitar played a slow sorrowful bridge, making them wait for the answer. Then he painted yet another picture.

I dreamed I saw a river, where the water was deep and clear
Then a single drop of rain made my reflection disappear…

Finally, the man in the story understood. The audience sighed involuntarily at his revelation, rejoicing with him.

Now I'm list'ning for angel singing, when I wake up each day
I stop to look for miracles everywhere along the way…

The song finished.

And Lord, we sure could use a miracle today.

Sonny pushed his cap back and grinned.

There was no reaction.

There were thirty or more people in the long narrow room; not a single person applauded. No one lifted a bottle; no one spoke.

Sonny shrugged. He pulled his cap forward and turned his eyes back to the frets of his guitar. He played the haunting 'Am'-'Em'-'D' opening to his other song about angels, the one he'd played earlier. He drew a picture again with his strings: the dark night, a weary man, tired from a long day, hurrying to beat the storm home.

I pulled in the drive, under stormy skies…

This time when Sonny finished and made his 'Aw Shucks' ball cap gesture, there was applause—boisterous, spirited applause! Joel and the girl singer, Toni, were on their feet.

But the clapping died as quickly as it had started. Conversation erupted. After being still for the duration of Sonny's songs, the audience exchanged enthusiastic commentary.

"The reflection thing…about the angel in the mirror? That was so clear, I could see it!"

"Looking through the windows, through the angel's eyes…that's what I liked!"

"'We sure could use a miracle today', that was like church, back home!"

****

Joel made his way to the stage. As he moved forward he could see that the guy was exhausted; it was all the older man could do to sit on the stool and smile. Joel hurried his steps.

"Great job, Jacob!" he said into Sonny's microphone. "I think we all had a little church here this evenin'. What do y'all think?" he asked the crowd.

There was hardly any response. People were still caught up, remarking to each other about the pictures the singer had painted, about the haunting quality of his guitar playing.

Joel leaned into the mic. "Hey folks!" he yelled. "Jacob, here, is gonna think y'all didn't like his songs if we don't let him hear from us!"

That brought applause, but it was half-hearted. Sonny stood and put his arm on Joel's shoulder. "Thanks, everyone," he spoke softly into the microphone. "That was fun."

He turned away from the audience and reached down to unplug the Stratocaster and make adjustments to his controller. Immediately feeling better, he turned back to Joel. "How about that duet you and Toni promised, Joel?"

****

Joel took it from there.

Toni's alto was a nice fit with Joel's strong tenor lead. They did Vince Gill's "When I Call Your Name," and "Pocket Full Of Gold," and then finished with the new Allison Crouse and Brad Paisley hit, "Whiskey Lullaby."

Jenny and Sonny enjoyed the songs, applauding enthusiastically with the rest of the patrons.

"Looks like 'open mic' will be cut a little short tonight," Joel announced when they finished. "Anyone else going to come up, John?"

John shook his head.

Joel turned to the female singer. "You and the Country Connection gonna finish off the evenin' downstairs, Toni?"

"We sure are, Joel!" she answered. She smiled at him and then at the audience. "My band's got another whole set to go downstairs, folks! Y'all come and join us down there!"

While Jenny gathered their coats, Sonny went to retrieve his guitar from behind the bar. "Thanks, again!" he yelled to John Tyler. "I really enjoyed playing that Fender!"

John smiled and waved. "Good luck," he called, "nice job tonight." His hands were busy closing down the console.

Jenny studied her husband as he walked back toward her; it was quiet now that most of the crowd had moved downstairs. "You ready to go?"

His walk was steady, his expression still alert. "I guess..." He shrugged, looking around, taking it all in. "This has been fun."

Joel, having finished packing up his gear from the stage, was walking out with the dozen or so people he'd been sitting with. "Y'all go on ahead," he told them. "I want to have a word with these good folks." He gestured at Sonny and Jenny; and then turned back to his entourage. "I'll see y'all Wednesday evenin'."

As the group passed by, a few of them stopped to shake Sonny's hand. "Very nice," a couple of then said. "Wonderful songs!"

Jenny turned to Joel. "You and Toni did a really good job. Your voices fit very nicely. Do you sing together a lot?"

The cowboy singer smiled. "Thank you, Ma'am. We've known each other quite a while. With her strong alto, anybody would sound good."

"It was really good," Jenny said again, looking to see if Sonny was through accepting congratulations.

When the others left..."Joel," Sonny laughed. "When you went back up after...what's her name?" He looked his question at Jenny.

"Emma?"

Sonny nodded. "When Emma finished that..." he laughed again, self-consciously, trying to finish his thought. "I guess what she did was singing. Anyway, Jenny said she sure hoped I didn't have to sing after that! You saved us."

Joel smiled. "Emma *is* a little different," he agreed. "But she's got a whole lot of pull in this town; it's best to humor her. She gets my songs radio time when nobody else in town does, even if it is kinda after-hours. No tellin' when or where she'll show up. I keep a schedule on my website, so she knows where to find me; she knows I'll bring her up on stage."

Joel turned to greet John as he passed by, on his way downstairs. “Here’s the culprit,” he said. “Did you listen to that tape before you played it?” he asked.

John laughed. “Are you kidding? Once is enough.” He rolled his shoulders, looking tired after a long day. “I can’t say I care much for her…music.

“She’s got clout, though. Did you see the size of the crowd with her? There must have been five tables. Tootsies is always glad to accommodate Emma Emerson.” He nodded at them and started down the stairs. “See ya.”

“Say,” Joel said, addressing Sonny, “you met some of the group I was with?”

“Yeah, nice folks…”

Joel set his guitar case on one of the tabletops. “Can you set that down a minute?” He gestured at Sonny’s case. He did; Jenny pulled out a barstool and sat, too.

Joel noticed Sonny’s eyes wander, his attention wavering. “Listen, if this isn’t a good time…”

Sonny cleared his throat, pulling out a stool, keeping his balance against the tabletop as he boosted up. “Sorry,” he said. “I’m a little tired.” He waved his hand absently. “I guess I’m not used to all this.”

“Those folks are from the church I go to, Central Christian.” Joel picked up on his original train of thought. “That’s in Inglewood, up north of town. A bunch of them decided to skip the evenin’ service and come hear me sing. They were really impressed by your songs! We all were.”

He paused, getting to his question. “I was wondering. How did you get the idea for the angel song…the one with eyes that lit up the rooms of the house?”

Sonny cut his eyes to Jenny; he was too exhausted to answer the question. She picked up his signal. “There’s a guy in our church, in Sonny’s Sunday School class…”As she started to explain, she realized that proper introductions had not been made. She offered her hand to Joel. “By the way, I’m Jenny Jacobs. This is my husband, Sonny.”

Joel scowled momentarily at the name difference, then let the confusion pass—lots of performers used another name. “Nice to meet you both.” He shook Jenny’s offered hand; her husband was still distracted.

“Anyway,” Jenny continued. “The guy was a real workaholic. His being gone so much started taking a toll on his family. Without ever mentioning who the song was about...he sang the song for ‘special music’ at a Wednesday night service.” She smiled at the memory. “I think more than one father in the congregation wondered if the song were about him. A lot of Oak Ridge engineers are pretty hyper, hard-charging types.”

Joel was nodding, paying attention to Jenny’s explanation. “I do some writing myself,” he told her. “I guess I never had that kind of inspiration. I sure like that song, though.”

He turned his gaze to Sonny. “And the way you sang it, too.”

Sonny smiled his thanks, but didn’t respond verbally.

Joel changed subject. “Say, I need to hang around for a few minutes while Toni and her group finish their set. But I wish we could visit a little more, get to know each other.”

Jenny touched her husband’s hand. “We could use some coffee before we head back to Oak Ridge, couldn’t we, Hon?”

Sonny nodded.

“We had an early dinner across the street at that barbeque place,” Jenny said. “We could meet you over there. How long do you think you’ll be?”

Joel looked at his watch. “Shouldn’t be more than fifteen, twenty minutes. A lot of times in the winter they close early on Sunday night.” He reached to hand Sonny his guitar case as they stood to leave. “If y’all don’t mind staying around for a little while, we’ll meet you over there.”

Chapter 4

"That didn't take long," Jenny said as Joel and Toni sat down to join them.

Jenny and Sonny were at the same booth in the barbeque restaurant; even the same chatty waitress was working their table. "Joel Reed!" the girl exclaimed; she had rushed to the booth when she saw Joel and Toni come in.

"Hi, Karla. How ya doin'?" Joel smiled at her.

"And Toni?"

"Right, Toni Clarkston…Can you get us some coffee, Karla?" Toni gestured toward Joel as they sat down, stacking their 10-gallon hats in the space between them. "That okay?"

He nodded.

Sonny and Jenny had already finished off a couple of cream cheese pastries. "Bring me a big glass of milk," Sonny told the waitress.

But Karla was just getting started. "So, how y'all doin'? Where were you playin' tonight? Oh, y'all just sound so *good* together…Did you do the Clint Black song tonight, the one where he sings with his wife, that TV woman?"

"'When I Said I Do'," Toni answered. "No, we didn't have time for that one tonight. We do get lots of requests for that song, though."

"When did you hear us do it?" Joel was straining to be cordial.

"Across the street at Legends Corner…back in the fall. Y'all tore 'em up that night. I remember you sang…"

Thinking the girl might never wind down, Jenny interrupted, "Karla, we'd really appreciate those drinks."

The waitress glared at Jenny and started to press ahead with her conversation. "Joel, how's that Arts thing goin'? You were writin' a new song for them."

This time Joel interrupted. "Karla, honey, these folks are visitin' all the way from..."

"Oak Ridge," Jenny answered him, "just north of Knoxville."

"Yeah," Joel said, "from Oak Ridge. Anyway, Karla, we'd like to spend a little time with them. You think we could visit afterwhile?"

"Well, sure, I guess..." The girl stabbed a glance at Jenny. "No problem."

Then she showed Joel her teeth. "Two coffees, right?"

"And a large milk..." Joel flashed his boyish grin. "Thanks, Karla. We'll sit down and have us a nice visit, real soon."

"I'll look forward to visiting, too," Toni added diplomatically,

Joel made the introductions as the girl shuffled away. "Jenny and Sonny Jacobs, this is Toni Clarkston."

Toni nodded at Jenny. "Hey, Jenny."

"Nice to meet you, Toni."

Toni saw that Sonny was—as Joel had warned on their way over—pretty much out of it. His elbows were resting on the table, his chin cupped in his hands. "Hey, Sonny," she said to be polite.

Sonny blinked his eyes but didn't move his head.

"I really enjoyed your songs," she said, hesitating. "So it's 'Sonny'? How did John get 'Jacob'?"

Jenny slipped her hands under her husband's elbow, nuzzling his shoulder. "I'm afraid today has taken a lot out of him. It's been a very long afternoon and evening."

"I understand, completely," Toni assured her, smiling at Sonny. "I get that way myself sometimes. Do a couple of gigs in a day and you catch yourself coming and going."

Jenny explained about the name confusion. "You know how sometimes you make introductions using your last name first? Well, the barmaid-slash-manager asked Sonny his name but walked away before he finished. So now he's Jacob, I guess."

"Things like that happen all the time; names kinda come and go in this business." Toni paused. "Oh, and her name is Susan, by the way. The barmaid, I mean."

"Right, Susan," Jenny said. "She looks awfully young to be the manager of a Honky Tonk."

Joel laughed. "We all try to look a little younger if we can pull it off."

"Anyway, we're glad you asked us to stay and visit." Jenny smiled at Joel. "It *has* been a long day, but it sure has been interesting."

****

Karla made her way toward them with her serving tray. "Coffees all around," she announced, setting cups in front of Joel and Toni, refilling both Sonny and Jenny's cups, "...and a large milk for the man in the baseball hat."

Sighting the bulge in Sonny's shirt pocket as she set his milk in front of him, Karla pointed, nearly touching his controller. "Hey," she said to Joel and Toni's side of the booth, "did he show you his thingy?"

They looked at her.

"It's like a TV remote thing for his pacemaker," the waitress informed them.

"Karla," Sonny said; a chill in his voice.

"Yeah?" She smiled.

"Give it a rest!" he growled. "We're trying to have a conversation here."

Karla looked at Joel, seeing if he would come to her defense. He did not. "Well, excuse me!" she grumbled, and turned on her heel.

"Sorry about that," Sonny said to the others. "Enough is enough. Where were we?"

"Long day..." Toni prompted, ignoring Karla's observation about Sonny's pacemaker.

Joel interrupted. "If y'all don't mind," he said, bowing his head. The others bowed as well. "Lord, we thank you for this sustenance and for this opportunity for fellowship. Bless those gathered at this table, in Jesus name."

There were 'Amens' all around.

Jenny let go of Sonny's arm to open a packet of sugar for her freshened coffee. "Thank you, Joel," she said, acknowledging his blessing. "It has been interesting, like I said. For instance, we didn't know what to make of the audience's reaction."

"The reaction to your first song was weird, Jacob," Toni said, "er…I mean, Sonny." Getting no response from him, she turned her gaze to Jenny. "I don't know as I've ever seen a crowd just clam up like that."

She paused, sipping her coffee as she thought about it. "I think the song was so unexpected. You come to a place like Tootsies and you get a certain kind of music, mostly hacks like me and Joel, mimicking the latest Country hits. That's what people expect.

"That song…" Toni nodded over her cup. "The one that started out with a prayer. Well, it was different."

She hadn't meant that the way it came out. "Don't get me wrong, they loved it. They absolutely loved it!" She turned to Sonny. "Where did you come up with such a unique idea for a song?"

Jenny nudged Sonny's leg. He still had his head cupped in his hands, staring into space. The nudge prompted him to gulp some milk. Without thinking about it, he reached into his pocket and beeped twice, wanting to feel a little more alert. He left the controller lying on the table. "It's called 'Bev's Song'. I wrote it about Beverly Rivas, a friend of Jenny's.

"She was on the list for a liver transplant. It was gonna take a mir…miracle to get the transplant in time to save her life." He rubbed his right eye, feeling nauseous, but wanting to hold up his part of the conversation. "The song was to remind us that miracles come in a lot of different forms."

"All of Sonny's songs are about people we've known," Jenny added, melancholy in her voice, "things that have happened in our lives."

Joel couldn't ignore the controller, there on the table—he had to ask. "What does the beep mean? Are you sure you're alright?" He gestured at the device, genuinely concerned.

Sonny finished his milk and took a sip of his coffee. He touched the area beneath his collarbone. "I have an implant. It's not a pacemaker. It's a power pack for a neuro…neuro…" Flustered, he shortened his answer. “I have a wire back here, to help manage pain.” He gestured at a spot on the back of his neck.

“Wait…” Toni interrupted his explanation, asking Jenny, “what about your friend, the one who needed the miracle?”

Sonny shook his head, glancing at his wife. “There’re lots of different kinds of miracles, Toni.”

There was a momentary silence, each person at the table studying his coffee cup, thinking about the nature of miracles. Joel finally broke in. “See, Toni. That’s Sonny’s hook.”

“His what?” Jenny asked.

Toni turned to Joel, as if only the two of them were at the table. “Yeah, you’re right.” She sipped her coffee again, giving Joel’s idea time to sink in. “That’s what everyone in the room wanted to know, wasn’t it? The person who saw the angel in the river…did he get his miracle?

“The song was unique,” Joel added, “but there was something about the *way* he sang it, too. Did you feel that?”

Sonny and Jenny watched Toni reflect for another moment, and then Toni painted a picture of her own: “Guy in a ball cap, no big belt buckle, no fancy hair style.” She absently fingered a lock of her dark hair curled around her right ear. “Pulls the hat down, all serious, doesn’t say a word, just plays a chord and breathes a prayer into the mic.”

“Fingers going like crazy…” Joel added to her description, “…doesn’t look up. Looks like it *hurts* to tell us the story—makes us *want* to listen, all the way to the end!

“Then he pushes back the hat and waits, still doesn’t say a thing. Like: ‘I’m singing about angels and miracles, take it or leave it’. And when they don’t respond to…” He paused again. “…to his music, his lyrics—his story—he tugs down his cap and starts another one.”

They both turned to Sonny; this time Toni spoke. “Keep the ‘Jacob’, it fits with the stories—kinda Biblical. You should just do your thing, Jacob.” She nodded, satisfied with their analysis. “On stage, on the tube, wherever there’s an audience. You’ve got your hook, go sell it!”

Joel laughed and nodded his agreement. He turned again, looking for Karla. “I’ve got time for one more cup, but then I’ve got to get on home.”

****

Karla noticed Joel turning in his seat; she grabbed her coffee pot and hustled to their table. "If I'm not interrupting..." Karla smiled at everyone. She poured a fresh cup for Joel and looked at her other customers. Jenny moved her hand toward her cup. Sonny and Toni shook their heads. "Can I get anyone a piece of chocolate cake? We've got some fresh strawberry pie."

Joel asked for the pie. He reached in his jeans pocket and pulled a business card from his wallet, handing it to Jenny. "Have you got a pen and some paper in your purse?"

Jenny studied the card. "'JoelReed.com'...you have your own website?"

Toni retrieved one of her cards from her oversized saddle-leather purse and handed it to Jenny. "It's an absolute necessity, Jenny." She nodded at her own card. "That one is for my band, Country Connections. A website let's your fans keep track of where you'll be appearing, any new releases, whatever."

Karla returned and placed Joel's pie in front of him without comment. "Thanks, Karla," he said.

"Write down your email address for me and I'll send you a couple of contacts," he told Jenny. As she fished around in her purse for some paper, Joel nodded at Sonny. "Alright if I pass it on to John Tyler, the soundman at Tootsies? He's got his own studio—he might be able set you up with a demo."

Sonny took an audible breath, willing himself to expend the energy to pay attention. He heard Joel's question, but he just couldn't muster an answer—his neck was radiating a message: *Rest, now!*

He reached to adjust his controller, but thought better of it. He put his chin back in his hands. Stabilizing his neck kept his chin from dropping—kept the high amperage from stinging. "We're getting in over our heads..." he whispered to Jenny.

Sensing Sonny's discomfort, Joel took a couple bites of his pie, giving the couple time. He wrinkled his nose. "Not too fresh...strawberries in winter, I should have ordered the cake."

He hadn't understood Sonny's shortened explanation about the pain-control device but sensed that he was on his last legs. There was something unique about—Jacob, Sonny, whoever he was—his songs were special. Joel had to know more; he needed to find a way to stay in touch, to somehow get involved with this music. *Lord willin',* he said to himself.

"What do y'all do in Oak Ridge?" Joel asked aloud. "I mean, how does it happen that you're singin' at a place like Tootsies? Kinda different from your usual religious performances, isn't it?"

Jenny looked up from her writing. "Oh no, we're, er…I mean, Sonny's not…He has sung some 'special music' for church, but it's been a while."

"I thought…" Toni said.

Joel nodded. "Me too. You mean you're not a performer? I thought you were tryin' to expand your fan base—out from, let's see, Oak Ridge is East Tennessee. I figured you for a Bible-belt singer, Sonny. County fairs, Christian music festivals, stuff like that."

"I'm a high school science teacher and coach," Sonny managed to reply. "Jenny's a bookkeeper."

"'Coach Jacob', that's even better!" Toni proclaimed. "That explains the ball cap. CeeCee would love you, a singin' coach with a name from the Bible. Great! More of your hook…"

"Who's See-See?" Jenny asked.

"What's a 'hook'?" Sonny asked at the same time.

Joel laughed at Sonny's question. "Your hook means your *thing*—your niche, what sets you apart."

He paused, introspective. "Ever since I was a kid in Fresno, I knew I'd play guitar and sing. It's all I've ever wanted to do. Toni called us 'hacks' while ago; that's partly right, I guess. I can play anything I hear, and I sound a lot like Glen Campbell. But there's already a Glen Campbell."

Toni got caught up in the storytelling. "My real name is Rhonda Bixwell…" She laughed spontaneously, along with the others. "Yeah, it's a funny name. I've tried Tina Johnson, Reva Jones…Now, since Terry Clark made it big, I let my hair grow and voila! I'm Toni Clarkson."

"Are you a couple?" Jenny asked.

Joel touched the girl singer's hand and smiled. "We've been 'buds' since the old Opryland days, but no, we're not together. I married my high school sweetheart. I have a daughter, Kasi, she's thirteen now."

"I've been divorced for a year or so," Toni said. "The band takes up all my time these days. Tootsies is one of three places my band is playing, right here in Nashville."

"So tell us more about this 'hook' idea," Jenny said.

Rhonda Bixwell laughed at her confusion. "Think of it this way. Remember Joel's song for the Arts Council?"

"Yes, I liked it very much!"

Toni continued. "That's an example of a hook. Joel's trying to promote his songwriting and performing in a new way, a new style for him. See if he can establish an identity, something to set him apart; make him different."

Jenny nodded, paying attention.

"Well, your husband *is* different. The ball cap, not saying anything, the angry, determined look he gets when he plays. All that and those *great* songs! That's all part of his hook!"

"And who is See-See?" Jenny asked her other question again.

Toni pointed to Jenny's pen and paper, spelling it for her. "It's C-E-E, C-E-E. BeeBee and CeeCee Winans are big in Gospel and Christian music. Surely you've heard 'Hallelujah to the King'? It's on her 'Throne Room' album."

"Toni sang backup for the Winans," Joel said. "When, Toni? Late nineties?"

Her face lit up. "I did a studio gig with them on their 'Heaven' album. It was a long time ago." She tried to make light of it, but Jenny could tell the project had been a career highlight. "Once upon a time, I was under contract, back in my Reva Jones days."

Joel pushed the remainder of his pie aside and took a last sip of coffee. "I gotta git, as they say here in Nashville!" He stood and put his hat on, shrugging into his jacket. Pulling a money clip from his front jeans pocket, he began unfolding the bills.

"Oh, Joel, we've got the tab," Jenny said. "Please, it's been so nice visiting with you both." She tore off the bottom half of the paper she'd been writing on and handed it to him.

He put away his clip and reached for the slip of paper, winking at Jenny. "It's been great; we have to keep in touch!"

As Toni slid out of the booth, gathering her white cowboy hat, she asked, "Where are you parked?"

"In the Ryman's lot…you?"

"Clear up on Tenth. I was runnin' late, the guys gave me a ride down in the equipment van. You can give me a lift back to my car."

Joel nodded at Jenny. "How about y'all? Did you park close?"

Jenny waved her hand. "We're fine. You go on ahead. Awfully nice talking with you both! We'll be checking your websites, come to hear you play sometime." She nudged Sonny, under the table.

"Ungh!" He grunted, and then brightened. "It really was great!" He struggled to his feet and shook Joel's hand.

When he reached to shake Toni's hand, she pushed it aside and gave him a hug. "I expect to see you on the GAC network real soon, Jacob! We'll be looking for that angel song on the Gospel charts, too."

Sonny smiled as she pulled away. "I enjoyed your singing." He included Joel in his bleary-eyed gaze. "Thanks for everything."

Slipping Jenny's paper into his pocket, Joel took a step forward to grasp Sonny's shoulder. "I'll be prayin' for you, brother; you and your music. I think your songs are gonna touch a lot of hurtin' hearts."

Sonny didn't turn away, he met Joel's gaze head-on. "I appreciate that, Joel."

Joel helped Toni with her coat; then curled his fingers around the handle of his guitar case, there on the floor at the end of the booth. "You ready?"

Toni nodded and they were gone.

****

Jenny called a cab to carry them back to the end of Second Avenue, where they'd parked. As she started the car, she glanced at the dashboard clock. 9:15. "That's a surprise," she commented as Sonny adjusted his seat to rest. "Seems like its midnight, don't you think?"

"Ungh," her husband replied.

Chapter 5

Sonny prepared tomato soup and grilled cheese sandwiches for Monday's lunch.

"I thought you'd still be in bed, Hon," Jenny remarked as she came into the kitchen. She had just come in, wearing a pink smock, the uniform for her Monday morning volunteer duties at the hospital.

"It's been…what, almost two full months since the implant, Jen? I'm exhausted from yesterday's trip, but I've got the settings figured out pretty well. I'm doing alright." He grinned at his wife. "Truth is, though, I didn't get up until after eleven."

Jenny took a bite of her sandwich. "Hot off the grill, huh?"

He nodded.

"Sonny, you should have seen this family in the waiting room this morning. I bet every one of them weighed over three hundred pounds. Their mother was having a bypass, so I can't blame them for looking kinda skuzzy. But, smell? You could almost see a green fog of sweat coming out of their corner."

Sonny hadn't touched his food; staring vacantly out the window, he didn't acknowledge her story.

Jenny touched the back of his hand. "You should eat something." She sighed, tapping his wrist when he didn't stir. "Sonny?"

He shook his head and took up his spoon, sipping at the soup, and then reached for his controller, making a two-beep adjustment. Still unfocused, he started eating his sandwich.

****

After their quiet meal—eating perked Sonny up a little—the couple went out to the back yard. The sun was bright, but the cold wind they'd felt in Nashville had followed them home. Sonny found Fred's old towel from the workroom under the porch and played tug-of-war with his dog. Huddled in her jacket, Jenny found a yard refuse bag and made the rounds of their planter boxes, scraping out dead roots, working the potting soil loose in preparation for new flowers.

"Did you check the mail?" Jenny asked. They were back in the kitchen; water for coffee was warming in the teakettle.

"No, I didn't even think about it. You get it, I'll fix the coffee."

As he stirred creamer into their instant coffee, Jenny sorted through envelopes and junk mail. "Something from Intercom," she commented, opening it.

Intercom Insurance was the company that provided Sonny's disability compensation. Jenny hesitated as she started reading this correspondence, but her husband was waiting for her to tell him what it said. "They're requesting something called a 'Consultative Examination'. Apparently, Intercom is paying for it. They've already made you an appointment with someone named Tracy L. Greene, EDD."

Sonny set their cups on the table and plopped into his chair. "Con…?"

"Right, that's what it says, 'Consultative Examination'."

"Can they do that?"

"What?"

"Make me go to a nut doctor?"

"Sonny…"

"Well, I'm not going."

Ignoring his stubbornness, Jenny continued studying the letter. "The office is on Emory Lane, that's right off Emory Valley Road. The appointment is for three o'clock, Monday, March twenty-first."

She looked at the wall calendar. "Wait! That's today!"

Sonny laughed. "No way."

"That's what it says. Typical insurance company, not sending the notification until the day of the appointment."

She studied the information at the bottom of the form. “There’s an eight-hundred number. I’ll call them and get it straightened out.”

Sonny got up and started into the other room. “I’m gonna go lie down.”

The insurance company stonewalled Mrs. Jacobs. Yes, the appointment *is* set for 3:00 pm, Monday the 21st. Yes, it *is* unfortunate that the correspondence didn’t give more advanced notice. Is there a specific health reason for Mr. Jacobs not keeping the appointment? There are to be no exceptions! Unless Mr. Jacobs obtains a doctor’s certification stating that he is physically unable to keep the appointment. It is mandatory and will not be changed.

“You have nice day, too,” was Jenny’s sarcastic last word. *Stupid bureaucracy! Today of all days!* Sonny was dead on his feet.

She reached behind her shoulder for the address book on the baker’s rack, thinking to lookup the number for the school system’s administrative offices. She placed the book back without opening it; the school system wouldn’t be able to change the appointment, especially on such short notice.

The clock on the stove read 12:25. She could let her husband rest for a couple of hours before informing him that the appointment had to be kept.

****

The outer door of Dr. Greene’s office opened to a modest waiting room. Sonny tried to see through the frosted glass panels into the receptionist area, there was no light or noise back there. Finding the single interior door locked, he knocked. No answer.

The doctor was late; he checked his watch. 2:53. Well, she wasn’t actually late yet, but he resolved to leave if she wasn’t back by exactly three o’clock. He settled into one of the two chocolate-brown upholstered chairs. There were no magazines on the oak end table between the chairs, only a small single-speaker FM radio. Elevator music from EZ-88.3 was playing softly.

The straight-backed chair was uncomfortable. He stood up and paced around the tiny waiting area, studying the wood-grain pattern of the floor and then peeking through the blinds to check the parking lot.

The only vehicle to be seen was the one he'd driven, Jenny's blue '94 Ranger. He fiddled idly with the radio, finding WIMZ 103.5 and cranking up the volume on "Sweet Child Of Mine. " Mounted on the wall he noticed a clear-plastic display case containing several pamphlets. A Living Well Seminar would be held at the Oak Ridge Senior Center on April 15th, to be facilitated by Tracy L. Greene, EDD.

"Facilitated!" Sonny harrumphed.

His neurostimulator was turned way up; every time he lowered his chin he received an extra-strong jolt, just to remind him what kind of day he was having. He was still fidgeting, drumming his fingers on the receptionist's marble counter top to "Sweet Home Alabama," when the outer door opened.

A tall, thin woman with dark shoulder-length hair and a severe expression walked directly to the radio, turning the sound down. Without so much as a glance in Sonny's direction, she used her key to unlock the inner door, quickly squeezing through, flicking a light switch and closing the door behind her.

"Well, so nice to meet you, too," Sonny grumbled. He took a long stride and stood directly in front of the inner door, his large body filling most of the space beneath the doorjamb. It was an inward opening door; he waited with his arms crossed. Aggressive body language!

In just a moment, the door swung open. "Oh," the woman said, finding herself looking up into Sonny's face. She gave him her professional I'm-in-charge-here smile. "You'll have to excuse me," she told him, gesturing for him to move aside.

He took a step back, returning her phony smile but not saying anything, maintaining his antagonistic posture. He'd been a coach a long time; this wasn't his first battle of wills.

The doctor walked over to reset her radio to the easy-listening station. Satisfied that she had reclaimed her territory, she turned; her chilly expression still intact. "You're Mr. Jacobs?" she asked, gesturing for him to precede her through the inner door. "My office is just inside, to the left."

There was a cluster of chairs around a small circular table in a corner to her left. She nodded her head to the right. "Have a seat in front of the desk, if you will."

Sonny took the nearer chair, pulling it a couple of feet away from the edge of her desk before sitting down and crossing his arms again.

Dr. Greene took her seat behind the desk. There were several files scattered on the top, and a framed picture: a distinguished husband in a 3-piece suit, two teenage kids whose features favored their mother, posing in front of the family fireplace.

The doctor made a show of shuffling the folders, saying "Ah..." upon finding the one bearing Sonny's name.

She tapped the folder, there in front of her, but didn't open it. "I'll be making an evaluation," she began without further ado, "and I'll be submitting my findings to the Disability Compensation department of Intercom Insurance, as requested by their office."

She paused for several seconds, looking directly into Sonny's eyes.

He didn't blink.

"Well, let's get started." She opened his folder and clicked a ballpoint pen, touching a line on a sheet of paper inside the folder, apparently some sort of checklist.

Sonny stretched his legs, placing the toes of his running shoes against the bottom edge of her desk. He ran both hands over his eyes and let out a long sigh. He was nauseous, he was tense—he needed to lie down.

The pulse from his stimulator wasn't strong enough. He stood up, pulling the controller from his shirt pocket, beeping. He glanced down at his shoulders, willing the current to increase and ease the throbbing.

He walked away from the desk, pacing around the conference table, too jittery to remain seated. *I give up; you win,* Sonny sighed to himself, his back to his adversary. The battle of wills was over. He was too tired to compete any more with the doctor, and too sick.

"'Radiation induced neuropathy'..." she read from her folder, ignoring his moving about. "Were you involved in an accident at one of the plants?"

Despite himself, Sonny laughed. "Nah," he answered, turning toward her. "That's good, though," he allowed, "here in Oak Ridge and all."

The psychiatrist backed her chair away from her desk at arms length, the pen still in her hand. Sonny studied her apparel: tan silk blouse over brown wool slacks—casual, but still professional. The professor of his Psychology of Coaching class, years ago, had noted that brown was a soothing color.

He beeped again, glancing down, and then looked back at her. "But no, I work for school system, not at one of the plants. I had cancer a while back. They used a high dos…dosage of radiation to kill off the bad cells after my operation. Now, years later, it's biting me."

Her face relaxed a little, responding to his lightened mood. "And the pain is where?"

"It's here…" He gestured with his left hand at his neck and shoulders. He abruptly grasped the back of one of the chairs in the cluster, the nausea making him slightly dizzy.

Turning the controller in his right hand, so that she could see it…"This beeper is a remote. I have an implant that sends an override current up my cervical spine." He shrugged. "Works pretty good, sometimes."

"I can see you're quite uncomfortable. Is the pain severe?"

He walked back over, slumping into the chair. "I should be in bed, really. It's a rough day." He looked down at his feet, stretching his legs forward again.

"Hard to concentrate," he told her.

She pulled back up under the desk, readdressing the papers in front of her. "This won't take too long. You're welcome to walk around, do whatever you have to. I have some questions, but they don't require that you sit still."

"Okay."

"You say this is a bad day. Why don't you describe a typical day for me? What are your daily activities? Why don't you compare a good day to a 'rough' day, in terms of your activities?"

Haltingly, with questions for clarification interjected by Dr. Greene, Sonny outlined his days for her, hour by hour: his good and bad days, including references to his daily walks, his frequent naps. He lost his train of thought a couple of times and found himself pacing again. "I'm kinda distrac…" he said at one point, "dist…I'm not too alert."

"That's fine," she said, her voice calm, reassuring. "Take your time."

When he returned to his seat, the doctor paused; then began a more direct line of questioning. "Mr. Jacobs?"

"Yeah?" He looked up at her.

"I'm going to list three items. I want you to remember them. I'll ask you to repeat them later, okay?"

"Sure, go ahead."

"A car, a book, and a tree. Would you repeat those, please?"

"Car, book, tree," he parroted, rubbing his nose, trying to concentrate.

"Fine," the doctor said. "Now, repeat these numbers for me: two, six, three, seven, nine."

He repeated the numbers without hesitation.

"Good," she said, making a mark on the paper in the folder. "And what is today's date…the day and the date?"

Sonny thought for a minute. "Monday, March the…it's nearly the end of the month; I know, because our team is playing Clinton at home today at five." He remembered Jenny looking at the calendar and commenting earlier, but couldn't recall the actual date. "Twenty-something, I don't know: twenty-first, twenty-second?"

"And the year?"

Sonny let out a breath in exasperation. "Two thousand five," he answered, "…in the year of our Lord."

"And who is our current President?"

"'W'…" He sighed. "George W. Bush." His expression suddenly clouded. "Hey wait! I forgot the three words, tell me again." He tried a disarming smile but he was genuinely concerned, he couldn't recall even one of the three items she'd told him to remember.

"That would be cheating." She returned his smile. "I can't tell you."

Sonny pulled his feet up under his chair, leaning forward suddenly. "Tell me!" he snarled.

The doctor's placid demeanor didn't change at the outburst. She looked intently at him, waiting for him to calm.

"Sorry," he said, sitting back. "Look, I forgot those three words. If you don't tell me them again, I'll fail your little test."

She nodded, good-naturedly. "Okay: a car, a book, and a tree."

"CBT," Sonny said, struggling to pay attention, to get it right. "Car, box, tree…car, box, tree."

The doctor didn't correct him. "Mr. Jacobs, name the Vice President. Oh," she continued without letting him respond, "also: your mother's maiden name."

"CBT," Sonny muttered before answering. "Al Gore and Eleanor Engleton…CBT," he repeated. He beeped his controller again, feeling conspicuous; then stretched his legs in front of him.

"Let's work with some numbers," the doctor said patiently, reclaiming eye contact whenever he would let her.

"Sure," Sonny said.

"What is the sum of twenty-six and seventy-seven?"

Sonny rubbed his right eye. "Car, box…" The doctor was looking at him, waiting for an answer to her math problem. "What were those numbers again?"

"What is the sum of twenty-six and seventy-seven?" she repeated.

"Ninety-three," he said, then immediately corrected himself, "no, a hundred and three."

Then, abruptly, he was agitated again. "Wait!" he said, leaning across her desk, "I said, 'Al Gore', while ago. It's Cheney, the heart attack guy. Gore was Vice President for Clinton." Sonny shook his head and returned to a normal sitting position. "God, I really need to lie down," he complained.

Offering her serene smile again, Dr. Greene made a point of checking another item on her list, making note of his revised answer. "Let's try that list of three items now, shall we?" she asked, catching his gaze as he raised his head.

Sonny smiled confidently. "Car, box and…" He stopped.

"Car, box…CBT: car, box, table!" He tried to sound confident. "Yeah, that's it: car, box, table."

"Fine." The doctor's expression was noncommittal. "Let's spend a few minutes talking about some of the responsibilities of your occupation. You're a school teacher?" she prompted.

Ordinarily Sonny was confident and enthusiastic about his job as a physical science and biology teacher. Today, his account was disjointed. "I teach freshmen and tenth graders, mostly. They like to mess with the pulleys and ramps. Darwin and evol...Darwin and evol..." He couldn't think of the word.

He made a few more comments, describing his teaching duties, sometimes stumbling over technical references. "You mentioned your team had a game today, against Clinton. You're a baseball coach, then?" the doctor prompted again.

Sonny nodded his head. "You know, if I can get past some of these bad days, I should be back in the dugout before the season is over."

The thought of returning to coaching gave him boost. For a few minutes he energetically described how his hands-on teaching technique in science labs was similar to the way he coached his baseball teams—always getting the kids involved, encouraging them to invest something of themselves in the learning process. He watched the doctor's face brighten as he talked; glad their conversation was finishing on a good note.

****

"I'll be sending my findings to Intercom," Dr. Greene told Sonny. Closing the folder, she rose and offered her hand as she walked around her desk and escorted him out to the reception area. "Thanks very much for coming in."

That went pretty well, Sonny told himself as he eased into the Ranger, careful to keep his neck straight, avoiding another bite from the electrode in his neck.

But on the ride home he was genuinely concerned. "'If I can get past these bad days...'" he mumbled, recalling his words to the doctor. *Will that ever happen?*

****

Taking advantage of her time alone while Sonny kept his appointment, Jenny did some computer research. JoelReed.com was a fascinating website. There were pictures, links to clips of Joel's recordings, a page with upcoming appearance dates, and a personal bio. The website for Country Connections wasn't nearly as complete.

Except for a nice picture of Toni with the band and a link to a sound clip, every menu selection led to a colorful icon proclaiming, 'Sorry, Under Construction'.

She used the email connection at each site to forward a 'Thank You' note, telling Joel and Toni how much she and Sonny enjoyed their time together and complimenting them on their creative websites. For Joel she picked a distant concert date that looked like it might fit into their schedule and said they'd try to come hear him sing.

****

"I said Al Gore was Vice President," Sonny told his wife when she asked how his appointment went. "But I tried to tell her I'm feeling pretty crummy today."

"I'm sure you did very well," Jenny reassured him.

He groaned, heading for the bedroom. "I'm gonna try to catch another nap before we go to the game."

"Other than that thing about the Vice President," he said, turning on the overhead fan and closing the blinds before stretching out on the bed, "I guess it went alright."

Chapter 6

"What did you mean, last night?" Jenny asked, absently clicking the TV remote in time for Final Jeopardy. "When you said we were getting in over our heads?"

They had just returned from watching the Wildcats lose a one-run game to the Clinton Dragons. "Money," he answered.

Jenny depressed the mute button, cutting off Alex Trebek as he read the clue. "It takes a lot. Business cards, websites, demos…"

"You'd have to go on Jeopardy for us to afford that stuff." Sonny leaned forward in his chair. "You think they'll really ever get back to us—Joel and Toni?"

"Sure, I think they were being genuine, wanting to encourage us.

"While you were at the doctors, I looked up their websites. I wrote both of them an email, thanking them for having coffee."

"Did you mark them in 'Favorites'?" he asked.

She nodded.

"Let's have a look."

Jenny flicked the remote to 'Off' and followed him into the computer room.

"This is pretty cool," Sonny remarked as he pulled up JoelReed.com. He clicked a music clip link labeled 'Claude Monet' and heard the familiar opening chords to Joel's Arts Council song. "That's the one he played last night." It was a short clip.

"Check out the 'Calendar' link. I put a note in Joel's email that we'd try to make it to one of his concerts." She touched one of the dates on the screen. "The Tennessee Theatre's over near the UT campus, right in downtown Knoxville."

"We could probably make that. It would be fun." Sonny paused a moment, a recalling the touch of Joel's hand on his shoulder, the sincerity of his appreciation for his songs. "That was awfully nice, didn't you think..." He sighed. "What Joel said about our music touching hearts?"

"It was." Jenny smiled, remembering, too. "He said he would pray for you, Sonny. And he said a blessing before drinking his coffee, not the least bit self-conscious about his faith."

"What did you think about *his* singing, Jen? I mean when he sang that Claude Monet number, not the Glen Campbell stuff. The song wasn't that great, but I liked his voice. I liked the harmony, too, with..."

"Toni."

"Yeah, with Toni, that was good. What did you think?"

Jenny pushed her hair away from the back of her neck, feeling warm in the small room. "It's hot in here. Turn on the fan."

Sonny reached up and pulled the chord to start the ceiling fan.

"His *real* voice," Jenny continued, "when he's not imitating somebody else, has that same openness, or maybe honesty, as your voice, Hon. I really liked his singing."

Sonny shrugged, turning back to the computer screen. "Let's look at Toni's site.

"Well, she said they were just starting out." He looked away from the screen. "Heaven only knows what it would take to get one of those up and going. Maybe I could get..." he hesitated.

"What?"

"The basketball coach—Jim. I could get Jim to build a web site for us; he updates all the school sports sites."

Jenny gestured at the screen. "I guess they use digital cameras and load in the pictures. Do you know anything about the sound clips, how they do that?"

"All we have is some diskette tapes that I made up...before, when I was entering all those contests. I think we'd need to make one of those demo things, a CD. Go to a recording studio. Like I said, we'd be getting in over our heads. We couldn't afford any of that stuff."

Sonny clicked the 'X' in the corner of their BellSouth Internet connection. He leaned back in the computer chair; Jenny was sitting on the daybed, against the wall. "We *did* learn a lot last night, though. You had to do most of the talking but I was paying attention most of the time."

She smiled, crossing her arms in concentration. "Eyes on the prize. Our goal was to see if an impartial audience would like your singing—everybody loved you—mission accomplished!"

"But breaking into the music business at my age would be rough, Jen, even if we could find a way to get around the expenses.

"I sure wish I *could* start a new career."

Jenny uncrossed her arms and leaned forward to study his face. "A new career?"

"Yeah, I realized tonight, watching the guys play. After that psychiatrist makes her report, I'll probably never coach again."

His despondent announcement shocked Jenny. She leaned back, giving him space, her voice softened. "What happened at the doctor's office today, Sonny?"

"A singing career might work out, Jen. Something that doesn't take a lot of brain power." He let out a faltering laugh. "You'd do all my TV interviews, I could just juice up the amps and sing—we'd be Big Time!"

Abruptly, he rose from the chair, knocking his knee against the open keyboard tray. "Ouch!"

"Sonny?"

He hurried out of the room, grabbing his coat out of the hall closet. Jenny didn't follow him. "I'm gonna take Fred for a walk around the block," he called to her.

****

After more than 30 minutes Jenny grew anxious; a walk around the block usually took less than 10. At 45 minutes she slipped on her coat. She didn't run, not wanting to come upon a neighbor or Sonny himself and appear to be upset, but she did walk fast.

At Don McNutt's house on Ulysses, almost directly behind their home, Jenny cut back her pace. She saw her husband sitting on the concrete front stoop of the next neighbor, the Huffmans. Fred had his head in his master's lap, enjoying having his ears rubbed.

"Let's go, you two," she called lightly, as she approached. The breeze had dissipated but the damp night air was chilly. "You'll catch your death of cold out here."

Sonny literally jumped up from the stoop. "Time's a-wastin'!" he said, dragging on his dog's leash, "Come on, Jen, we've got research to do."

****

He insisted that she bring a yellow pad down to the filing cabinet in her sewing room. "Let's see, how do we have this stuff filed? Under '401k' or…

"Here's yours: T. Rowe Price." He pulled the folder out and ran his finger down the page. "Balance as of December thirty-first is just over one hundred and fifty K. Got that?" He gestured at the writing pad in his wife's hand. "Write it down, Jen, one hundred and forty-eight thousand and change."

Jenny glared at him. "What are we doing, Sonny?"

Sonny sat down, cross-legged in front of the filing cabinet, and looked up at her. "I've got two choices: sit around and worry what some psy…what some *psychiatrist* thinks; or I can get up off my sorry butt and take advantage of this music situation while I still can!"

"Sonny?" She sat down on the loveseat, next to her sewing machine. "Why am I writing down the balance of my IRA account?"

Sonny shrugged, his expression told her he was stating the obvious. "Assets. You gotta spend money to make money. We need to find out how much we've got. Write down one-fifty."

He pulled out another folder. "Mine was under '401k'. I've got seventy-three thou. One-fifty and seventy-three is how much?"

She tossed her pen and paper on the other cushion. "I don't care how much it is. I'm not writing down anything, Sonny Jacobs, until you tell me what happened at that doctor's office!

"I can see you're upset and I *do* want to help, but you've got to tell me why we're doing this! And we're not *about* to rush out and spend any of our retirement savings on something that we haven't even *discussed*!"

He put the folders back, closed the drawer and rocked up to his feet. "That's all we need from down here," he told her, making his way back through the doorway. "Come on, we'll log on to the computer to get our bank balances. We can view our mutuals online, too."

****

Sonny used the pad on the computer desk to jot down '73,000' and '150,000' then pulled up the SunTrust website. "Jenny," he called, expecting she had followed him upstairs, "what's our SunTrust password?"

There was no answer.

He got up and peered out the computer room door. His wife was nowhere in sight. He picked up his cell phone and sat back down, dialing their home phone number. He heard the phone ring twice before she answered the sewing room extension. "Jen?"

She hung up on him.

****

Moving the pad and pen from the loveseat cushion to the floor, Sonny sat. He tapped his foot, not looking at his wife and not saying anything.

Except to open a sewing magazine, she'd hardly moved since he'd gone upstairs. *I've got all the time in the world* her body language told him.

I'm too far gone, he wanted to tell her. *I'll never be able to coach again!*

But he only stared straight ahead. His stress level called for a boost to the amperage, but he ignored the pain.

For more than half an hour, the couple sat, neither of them saying a word.

Sonny was trying to be pragmatic, facing up to his disability. Watching tonight's game from the stands had been agony; he realized how much he would miss suiting up and guiding his ballplayers from the third base coaching box. The visit to the psychiatrist's office had brought home what he'd feared for quite a while now. Mentally, he was losing it! *Hey, life goes on,* he told himself. It was time to start looking for a new way to bring meaning to his life, before it was too late.

Jenny had noticed his somber attitude at the ball game—he'd kept his scorebook without a word to anyone. At the time she figured it was left over weariness from last night. Now she surmised that he'd faced yet another disappointment at this afternoon's 'Consultative Examination'. His 'spend money to make money' comment could only mean one thing; he wanted to jump off the deep end, to spend whatever it took to dive into a career as a singer.

Her husband had warned last night that they were getting in over their heads. She was determined—that would not happen.

Chapter 7

Jenny Jacobs had two important phone calls to make early Tuesday morning.

She and Sonny had finally talked things through last night, about his visit to the doctor. He told her about his halting descriptions of good-versus-bad days and how he'd been inarticulate in describing his teaching and coaching duties. "I made simple math mistakes and flat flunked a short-term memory test," he said. He was certain that the psychiatrist's report would end his teaching career.

At the moment, Sonny was taking Fred for a morning walk, wanting to get out of the house.

Jenny's first call was to the office of Dr. Tracy L. Greene. She was surprised when Dr. Greene, herself, answered the phone. "My receptionist was in an automobile accident," the doctor explained, "nothing too serious. She should be back in another day or two. How can I help you, Mrs. Jacobs?"

"I'm calling to give you the name of our family doctor, Dr. Donald Gupta. His office is in the Family Clinic on Vermont Avenue."

"Oh yes, I know Dr. Gupta. Why are you giving me this information?"

Jenny took a long breath. Wasn't it obvious? "I'd like for you to forward your findings from yesterday's appointment to Dr. Gupta's office.

"Right away, if you don't mind. We'll be making an appointment to review them with him."

There was a pause. "I'm afraid that can't be done, Mrs. Jacobs."

"I beg your pardon?"

"Your husband's visit was requested by Intercom Insurance. You'll have to contact them."

Jenny's voice took an edge. "I want those records, Dr. Greene. I'll have an attorney down your throat with HIPAA papers by the end of the day if I don't get them."

"Your threats are duly noted," the doctor answered. "But as I'm sure your attorney will tell you, HIPAA rules don't really apply in this situation. I am *not* giving the information to any third party. I provided information, as requested, to the Disability Compensation department of Intercom Insurance, the party who initially requested the evaluation.

"Good day to you, Mrs. Jacobs!" she hung up.

Undeterred, Jenny found the number for the Oak Ridge Schools administration office. After spending two full minutes on hold, she was informed that Mr. Kingston, the insurance compensation administrator, would return her call as soon as he was available.

Her second important call was to a business in Harriman, Tennessee, about 35 miles west of Oak Ridge. The yellow pages listed, under 'Recording Services': Custom Sound.

Sonny had also apologized last night for his cavalier attitude about spending their retirement money. They agreed not to spend their 401k or IRA money, under any circumstance—besides, Jenny had pointed out, there was a 10% penalty for withdrawing funds before the age of 59½—but it wouldn't hurt to look into the expense of creating a demo CD.

"Hinkle Exterminators," a female voice answered.

"I'm sorry. I'm trying to reach Custom Sound, the recording service."

"Oh, that's us, too!" the woman hurried to explain. "Jerry's studios are right upstairs. How can we help you?"

"Good, you have a studio…So, my husband could bring in his guitar and make a CD?"

The woman laughed. “Sure thing. Jerry can supply backup musicians if you need anything like that. Is your husband ‘in the business’, as they say, have we heard of him?”

It was Jenny’s turn to laugh. “Not yet, but you will!”

“Well, that’s fine. What exactly can we do for you?” She paused. “Can I get your name?”

“Jenny Jacobs, it’s for my husband. My husband’s name is Sonny Jacobs. I don’t think we’ll need any other musicians.” She hesitated. “How does it work? Do you charge by the hour, or by the song, or what?”

“Our basic rate is sixty-five dollars an hour. Of course, it depends…”

“Wow!” Jenny exclaimed, thinking it would be much more. She quickly toned down her enthusiasm. *Don’t act like you just got off the turnip truck…*”Let’s set up an appointment, we’ll come and see what you have available,” she said.

“Certainly,” the woman answered.

They set a time for Wednesday afternoon.

Mr. Kingston, the school system administrator, returned Jenny’s call. “I’ll send you a form for your husband to sign, Mrs. Jacobs, requesting that Intercom forward a copy of the report to your family physician. Then you can go over the results with your doctor. The examining doctor was correct, though, we have to go through channels on this.”

“Thank you, Mr. Kingston, you’ve been most helpful.”

Chapter 8

"That kid with two last names carried you pretty far this season, Jim," Sonny remarked, later that Tuesday afternoon. "I thought this was going to be a rebuilding season for you guys? Opening round of State wasn't too shabby."

Jim Norton was the predictably tall, thin basketball coach at ORHS; Karen, his statuesque wife, a former cheerleader at East Carolina University, where they had met, taught second grade at Norwood Elementary.

Jim was free in the late afternoon now that his season was over. "Nick Daniels-Milaard, that's his name," he told Sonny, "he's gonna walk-on in football at UT. Good student, he could go about anywhere. I got him some division two offers in basketball but he's set on UT.

"We should be a little quicker next year, but we'll miss his big body on the boards."

"I appreciate you coming over to help me out, Jim."

"Hey, no sweat." He was seated at Sonny's computer terminal. "Windows 95, good Lord, Sonny, you're practically in the Stone Age here."

Sitting on the edge of the daybed, Sonny was watching over his friend's shoulder. "We just use it for email and checking sports scores. Can you build a website on this thing—one like Joel's? I don't want all that 'Under Construction' junk that's on the other one."

Jim had looked over the websites that Jenny marked under her 'Favorites'. Even JoelReed.com was fairly rudimentary; kids in his Level II class made more sophisticated sites as part of their class projects. He looked up from the monitor. "Let's not get ahead of ourselves. You need pictures, sound clips, stuff like that, before we're ready for Jacob.com.

"That still sounds weird, by the way. You're gonna use just 'Jacob', not 'Sonny Jacobs', huh?"

"They said it sounded biblical."

"Who said?"

"Joel and Toni, the two singers I was telling you about, the ones we met in Nashville." Sonny grinned. "Anyway, Jenny's got us set up with a sound studio in…" He struggled to remember the town. "…over near the Roane State campus."

"Harriman?"

"Yeah, Harriman. Jenny made us an appointment for tomorrow afternoon. Maybe I'll make a CD. She said it won't be too expensive, but I've got my doubts."

The basketball coach / computer science teacher turned back to the keyboard. "I'm going out to Microsoft.com and get you some free software. Assuming they have it for your antique Windows version."

Sonny understood the basics of downloading. With their BellSouth DSL connection, the process was completed in a few minutes. Jim pointed the cursor at the new 'Windows Media Player' icon on the desktop. "This will let you play WMA and MP3 files."

"MP3, that's what the kids use for their iPODs, right? What's WMA?"

Jim turned fully toward his friend. "Hey, you're pretty sharp today." He pointed at Sonny's shirt pocket. "That thing still working good?"

"Actually, I'm having a great day. Except for going to the game yesterday, I spent most of the day in bed. After our trip to Nashville, I was worn slap out. But I'm good-to-go today."

"I'm glad your trip went so well! So, someday, when you're on Christian Radio, I'll tell everybody, 'I knew him when'. What stations are around here?"

Sonny shrugged. "The only one I know is WYLV, it's called 'Love89.1'. There are a couple of AM stations, too, I think."

"89.1…I'll set one of my car radio buttons. You listen to it?"

Sonny laughed. "Never have. I guess I'd better start, huh? Check out the competition."

"You mean you never listen to Christian music; Michael W. Smith, Jars of Clay, Steven Curtis-Chapman, none of them? We had quite a few Christian stations back in Greenville when Karen and I were students at East Carolina; we used to listen to them all the time. It's pretty uplifting music."

He turned back to the computer. "Get out your credit card; we're going shopping at Wal-Mart."

Sonny stood up to pull his wallet from his back pocket. He watched as his friend dialed up Musicdownload.walmart.com. "I'll set a 'Favorites', while I'm at it.

"See, just put an artist in the 'Search' box." Jim entered 'Steven Curtis-Chapman' and began skipping down the list of singles available.

"Only eighty-eight cents?" Sonny grinned. "Show me how that shopping cart works. No, wait…"

He called to his wife, in the living room. "Jen, you should see this, we're about to spend some money on our MasterCard."

"The shopping cart is just like at the grocery store," Jim explained to both of them, Jenny standing behind him now, so that she could see clearly. "How about this one?" He pointed to 'All Things New'.

"Eighty-eight cents." Jenny chuckled, reading the price from the screen. "Aren't we big spenders?"

"Go for it!" Sonny was excited. "Show us how to use the credit card. I suppose it's…What's the word, Jen—nobody can see it?"

"Secure, you mean," Jim answered. "Yeah, Wally World is set up about as secure as you can get. We're logging in now." He reached to hand Jenny a pen and sticky pad from the desk. "Write down a password: 8 characters, numbers and letters."

She did. Jim made the entry, and then reached for Sonny's credit card and copied the numbers into the blank provided. "Now we verify that this is the song we want and download it."

As the download processed, he explained, "We're loading this song out into your 'Media Player' folder." In just a moment the software appeared on their screen and the song began playing, quite loud.

"Cool!" Jenny said.

"Way cool!" Sonny echoed.

Jim used the mouse to adjust the volume and looked at Sonny. "That's probably about all you need from me today, Coach." He turned to Jenny. "Where do you keep your CD's?"

"Down in the den, in the stereo cabinet," she answered. "Are we going to load them onto the computer?" She pointed to the CD slot at the top of their computer console. "Just stick it in the reader and the software will pick it up, right?"

Jim pushed the keyboard drawer back under the desktop and got up. "Yeah." He laughed. "That's all there is to it."

He looked at his watch. "Tell you what, sounds like you can figure that out for yourselves. I'll leave that to y'all, later on. I promised Karen I'd pick up the kids at the nursery."

Sonny walked him to the front door. "Thanks a lot, Jim. I'm sure I didn't get all that, but Jen and I will fool around with it."

Jim waved his hand, dismissing the effort. "You'll be able to load your CD after you record it in Harriman tomorrow. Then you can email songs to your producer or whatever."

"My producer." Sonny laughed. "Well, you've got us up and running. Are you sure that 'Media' software on my screen didn't cost anything?"

"Microsoft gives you free software so you'll buy other stuff." Jim turned to go. "See you later, Sonny."

"Yeah," Sonny said as his friend walked to his car, "I'll probably see you at the baseball tournament this weekend."

****

"Hey, come back in here!" Jenny called, still in the computer room. "We got a message from Joel."

They read it together.

From: Joel@joelReed.com
Date: Tuesday, March 22, 2005, 9:06 AM
To: Sonnyandjen@bellsouth.net
Cc: JohnTyler@tootsies.net
Subject: Re: Saying Howdy

Sonny and Jenny,
Nice to hear from you folks! Toni and I enjoyed visiting with y'all.
Glad you liked the website.
Here's the Southern Christian Music contact I promised:
Lynne Lewis RMG 615-322-8198—ext.12
Call her, email her, or meet and play a couple of your Christian songs.
I'm out the door. Hope to hear from you soon.
Happy day,
Joel

PS I forwarded your email address to John Tyler, the talent coordinator at Tootsies. I'm sure he'll be in touch!

"Too late to call his contact today, we'll try first thing tomorrow." Jenny smiled at her husband. "See, I told you he'd get back to us."

"That's great!" Sonny answered.

Chapter 9

"I've been thinking," Jenny told Sonny as he dunked a donut in his coffee Wednesday morning. "Let's call and play dumb at this RMG place. I think we should ask for some price quotes and see how they compare to the place in Harriman. It would cost us sixty-five bucks just to travel all the way to Nashville."

"What do you mean—play dumb?"

She sipped her Pepsi. "Remember we looked up RMG's website last night?"

He nodded. "Yeah, they had pages for about twenty different services. I'll bet they'll be pricey."

"Maybe we'll call their office." Jenny smiled. "Pretend we found them in the Yellow Pages. We'll see if they quote a high price or something reasonable. Play like we're fresh off the turnip truck."

Sonny giggled at the image. "I thought we were pretty much committed to doing our own CD, here locally—at the place in Harriman?"

"It won't hurt to get a quote to compare. I'll try RMG at ten our time, they're an hour behind.

"How many songs are you planning to do, at Custom Sound?"

"Three or four, I guess."

"And we're still agreed, right? We can afford about five hundred from our checking account, without going into savings."

Sonny beeped his controller once, responding to the stress of their decision-making. "So far, we've invested the grand sum of eighty-eight cents."

"What?" Jenny had her head in the fridge, pouring some more Pepsi.

When she closed the door, he rubbed his fingers together. "Eighty-eight cents, for the download."

"Oh, right, for that download Jim did from Wal-Mart." She laughed. "We're well under budget, so far." She took her drink and the newspaper into the living room.

****

"The price RMG gave me over the phone was, like, seventeen hundred bucks!" Jenny told Sonny as she drove through Oliver Springs, on their way to Custom Sound in Harriman. "They're going to send us a brochure."

"Wow! Compared to sixty-five an hour at this place?"

"Well, it was just like on their website, the price includes a bundle of services: their recording package, their distribution package, their promotion package…I asked twice for an hourly quote and the guy said that's not how their services are *packaged*. I told him I'd call back."

Sonny shook his head. "Fat chance."

In addition to his guitar, he brought a pile of Indian tablets—his lyric sheets. He had taken Fred for an early, short walk and then spent over an hour sifting through the song sheets, trying to decide what to record. "I've made up my mind. I'll do the two angel songs and 'Climb To The Mountaintop'. The 'Mountaintop' song will be a good change of tempo."

He tapped the pile, there in his lap. "Three songs should be enough." He hesitated, not wanting to get too hyped. "If we decide we can afford it."

****

The entry to Custom Sound was locked. Next door, through the glass of a converted storefront, they could see a matronly brunette beckoning to them.

"Hi, you're looking for Jerry?" she called as Sonny opened the door marked 'Hinkle Exterminators'.

The heels of Jenny's shoes echoed as she and Sonny walked to the rear of the large, mostly-empty room. The office area was delineated by a row of gray metal filing cabinets. "We have an appointment to see about making a recording," Jenny answered, "the door to the studio wasn't open."

A slender man, looking to be in his mid-50s, emerged from a doorway behind the receptionist. "I'll take this one, Rose," he told her and extended his hand to Sonny. "Jerry Hinkle…" The man wore pressed chinos and a long-sleeved white shirt, open at the collar; his graying hair looked to be razor-cut, his brown loafers were nicely polished.

Sonny shook his hand. "Sonny Jacobs. This is my wife, Jenny."

"Nice to meet ya." He nodded. There was a confident openness in Jerry's craggy face, honesty in the direct way his eyes met theirs. He gestured for them to follow him, pulling a ring of keys from his front pocket. "Let me show y'all the studio."

He unlocked the outer door and they followed him up a steep staircase. The dark wainscoted walls and plush blue carpeting on the stairs set an ambiance entirely different from the office they had just left. A walnut door opened to a serene paneled enclosure.

Jerry tapped a wall switch, bringing to light a professional control room with a large glass pane fronting the unlit studio to their left. The door to his office was to their right, at the end of a substantial black-leather couch. 'Whirlwind' was the label on the base of the sound console.

"This Control 24's state of the art," Jerry stated proudly, walking over to a set of switches at the base of a bank of electronic devices: cassette and reel-to-reel tape machines, a computer monitor, and various other components that neither Jenny nor Sonny recognized. He flipped some more switches, to illuminate the studio.

Walking back around to the studio door, he waved them inside.

There was a large black piano in the front of the low-ceilinged, well-lit room. Three microphones stands were on a raised, carpeted stage and there was a wide space to the rear, with a floor that looked like sand. Jenny walked over to the sand pit, where oversize amplifiers were spaced, facing toward the front. "Is this sand?" She knelt to take some in her fingers.

"Sure is."

Sonny touched the egg-carton surface of the off-white walls. "I've read about this," he said, "supposed to keep the sound from bouncing around or something."

"Right again." Jerry smiled, giving them time to take it all in.

Sonny strode to the middle microphone. "Testing, testing…" No sound came from the amplifiers. "I guess they're not on.

"Sure is quiet in here," he observed. "It's like its mu…mu…" He turned to his wife. "Jenny, what's the word?"

"Muted?"

"Yeah," he said, turning to the studio manager. "This is really cool!"

"Glad ya like it," he answered. "Do y'all both sing?"

"Oh no." Jenny smiled. "Sonny's the musician. I tell people I'm his groupie." Her eyes made a wide sweep of the room. "Have you seen what you need to see?" she asked Sonny.

He was back at the walls, feeling the texture again. He clapped his hands, listening. "This is like I pictured it." He gazed out through the glass panel. "You give me a thumbs-up and I start singing?" he asked Jerry. He noticed several high stools along the wall furthest from the entry door. "Could I pull one of those over when I sing?"

Jerry nodded.

"It's sixty-five dollars for an hour of recording, is that right?" Jenny wanted to know. "Are there charges for the CD?"

"Come on out and sit down and we'll visit a minute," Jerry answered. "Let me get a feel for what ya want." He looked at Sonny. "Did you bring a backup cassette or are ya gonna play?"

Sonny rubbed his eye, smiling broadly. "What? Oh, I was still in la-la land. This is just so…"

He moved toward the studio door. "I'll go get my guitar. You and Jenny can talk about money."

****

Sonny had to do two restarts on the "Mountaintop" song. The guitar fingering for the song had a bluegrass tempo. "I haven't played this one since…" he said into the microphone after the first take.

Jerry's accepting smile, through the glass, gave him confidence. "I've never tried it with the juice turned up." He touched his pocket.

"Sounded fine," Jerry said over the communication microphone.

"The chorus should be lighter, and I think I'll throw in an extra run at the beginning."

"Take your time, whenever you're ready."

With an intricate banjo-rhythm introduction, Sonny began again.

I need to climb to the mountaintop and praise the Lord
I need to raise my face to heaven, where the eagles soar
When this world becomes a burden I can bear no more
I need to climb to the mountaintop and praise the Lord…

****

"I can't wait to hear the playback!" Jenny said. "I couldn't hear a thing out here. It was like watching a mime." Sonny sat down next to her on the couch; she watched him unwind as he cut back on the amperage of his neurostimulator.

"Good stuff!" Jerry told them, setting his earphones aside. "Looks like you calmed some, Sonny." The studio operator's tone was casual, relaxed. "Is that what that gizmo is for?"

"Yeah, pain control," Sonny answered.

Jerry pushed a button and the first song that Sonny had recorded. "Angel With The Light In His Eyes," began.

Jenny felt comfortable with this amiable man—if this was the beginning of a business relationship, they were off to a fine start. She took her husband's hand and closed her eyes to listen as Sonny's voice emanated from the speakers, there amid the wall of electronic equipment. The first two songs were much as Sonny had performed them at Tootsies. There was a pure quality to the sound, as Jenny had expected, from a studio recording. Her husband's voice and guitar sounded every bit as good as any song on the radio.

After the two angel songs, Jerry skipped to the final version of the "Mountaintop" song. It was good, very good!

Sonny struggled to his feet when the songs were over. He was a demonstrative man—he often hugged the shoulders of his ballplayers—now he approached Jerry and prodded him to get up from his office chair. He grasped the man in an enthusiastic embrace. "Wonderful!" he exclaimed, "really, really great!"

"Thanks," Jerry said, waiting stiffly until Sonny finished the hug. "We don't usually get such good quality on the first go-round. Folks are usually self-conscious, tryin' to make up their mind on their arrangements. You seemed to get it right first try."

Sonny wasn't the least bit self-conscious as he stepped away from his new friend. "A place like this," Sonny began, but didn't finish. He walked over to gaze through the glass. "I've got eight or ten more I think are pretty good, Jerry. You make my songs sound like…Like I don't know? Pro…pro…"

"They sound *very* professional." Jenny finished his thought, rising from her seat.

Sonny paused a long moment before looking away from the studio, turning to face Jerry. "You asked about this, while ago," he gestured at the controller in his pocket. "I want to shoot straight with you.

"Jenny and I need somebody we can trust. We need someone like you, someone who's upfront, no BS. We want you to know what we're, what *I'm*, dealing with. Why I didn't practice the 'Mountaintop' song before we came." He reached for the controller, pulling it from his pocket. "I need to tell you about this."

Predictably, Sonny's adrenalin rush from the studio performance ran down quickly. He returned to the couch and began telling Jerry about his implant: how it worked to control his pain, how he had discovered its effect upon his music. But he wasn't able to finish his explanation.

He could feel himself tiring, but worse, he began stammering. "I have to stop, Jerry…I'm sorry, I'm not making much…

"I'd sure like to, you know, talk with you…" His smile was weak.

"…about *music*!" he said, too loud, thoroughly disgusted by his own weakness.

Jerry eased up from his chair behind the console. "We got a couple things done this afternoon," he said, including Jenny in his gaze. "I can cut this CD and have it ready in an hour or so."

Looking at Sonny, he revised his statement, no need to rush it. "Or anytime, whenever y'all can make it back." He smiled at Sonny. "Your music is first-rate, Sonny."

"How much do we owe you?" Jenny asked, finding her wallet, pulling out her MasterCard. "Your receptionist said you would take a credit card. We're trying to keep track of everything we spend on this venture."

"Sixty-five bucks," he answered, walking around to accept her card and reaching to turn on the light in his office. "This'll just take a minute."

"Is there an extra charge for the CD?" Jenny wanted to know.

"Need any copies?" he called from within.

"No, not right now, anyway. I sure hope we'll need more sometime..." She stopped mid-sentence, looking at Sonny.

He wasn't paying any attention; he had his guitar case in hand, eyes unfocused, waiting at the door.

Jerry shrugged when she didn't finish her answer and went about the business of processing the payment. His customers were obviously in a hurry to get away. "I'll be done in just a minute," he said.

Chapter 10

The ride back to Oak Ridge was enough for Sonny to recover from his tiredness. The recording session hadn't been nearly as stressful as performing; working with Jerry was almost relaxing. Restless when they got home, he decided to take Fred to Melton Lake Park for another walk.

"Want me to go with you?" Jenny offered.

"No, I'll take the Ranger. Fred and I will take a good, slow walk; give me a chance to think about things. We need to make a list of questions to ask Jerry. For instance, wonder how someone gets paid if they have a song on the radio."

He gathered his coat and Fred's collar. "That CD is gonna be really good, don't you think?"

"It sounded great when he played it back," Jenny answered, pecking him on the cheek.

She brought a Dolly Parton CD up from the basement and tried her hand at what Jim had shown them. Using the 'Copy From CD' menu item on the 'Media Player' software, she uploaded five songs from the "Little Sparrow" album. Paying attention to the directory selected by the software, Jenny sent an email message to Rachel Henson.

From: Sonnyandjen@bellsouth.net
Date: Wednesday, March 23, 2005, 4:38 PM
To: Drhenson@aol.com
Attachment: MyDocuments\My music\Shine.wma
Subject: Trying attachment

Rache,
No idea if this attachment will work.
I used Windows Media Player to load this song. See if you can play it on your computer.
Thanks,
Jenny

Following up, she called her buddy on the phone. "Hey Rache, check your email, would you please?"

Rachel, 'Rache' for short, was Jenny's best buddy. She and Doug had five children, ranging in age from 6 to 16. Jenny and Sonny were the Godparents of the two oldest Henson children, Greg and JoAnne. The two women spent lots of time together; shopping, bowling on the same team, just meeting for coffee. Only in her late-40s, but with twenty years service as a payroll supervisor at the Oak Ridge National Lab, Jenny had taken early retirement to help her husband cope with his health problems. Throughout Sonny's infirmity and various treatments, Rache had been Jenny's confidant and sounding board.

"What's up?" Rachel asked.

"I sent you a song attachment. Do you have 'Media Player' on your PC?"

"Yeah…"

"Well, I'm seeing if I can do this. Call me back after you try it."

"Jason's at soccer practice, I have to go pick him up in a half hour." She paused to look at the kitchen clock. "I guess I have time."

In a few minutes Rachel called back. "So?"

Jenny was in the kitchen. "Did it work alright?"

"Jen, it's no different than those weird joke attachments you send me all the time. What's so special about this song? I've heard it a hundred times."

Jenny left the dishwasher door open and sat down at the kitchen table. “Sonny cut a CD today!”

“He didn’t!”

“Yes, really. We went to a place in Harriman. We met this really nice guy named Jerry Hinkle; he has this great studio with egg cartons on the walls and everything.”

“So Jen,” Rachel interrupted, “why didn’t you send me a copy of Sonny’s CD?”

She laughed. “Oh, well, we didn’t get it yet. Jerry has to ‘cut’ it. But I was trying the email to see if I’d be able to send it to a Christian Country music contact that Joel told us about.”

“And Joel is…”

“You remember, I told you Monday morning about Joel and Toni?”

“Oh, right, I do remember.” She glanced at the clock again. “Look at the time; I’m gonna be late to get Jason. I’ll call you after dinner. You can fill me in on your…what did you call it?”

“I don’t know. It’s a Christian Country music producer or something. Listen, thanks for checking my attachment thingy. We’ll talk later.”

Jenny wanted to investigate one more thing before starting supper. She went back into the computer room and googled ‘WalMart’. At their site, under ‘Electronics’ she found a CD burner. A company named Iomega made one for $89.96. *We could afford that,* Jenny told herself. She’d have lots to tell Sonny over dinner this evening.

Chapter 11

"Small world," Jerry Hinkle told Sonny on Thursday afternoon. "So you know John Tyler?"

"Yeah," Sonny replied, "he's the talent whatchamacallit at Tootsies. The guy that runs the…soundboard; he's got something to do with what groups they hire, too. Nice guy."

"He still talk funny? Call ya 'Buddy'? Say 'youse guys'?"

"I didn't hear 'youse guys', but he did call me Buddy. He said he was from Chicago."

"When he first came down here, John and I worked runnin' lines and settin' up amps for concerts all over the southeast. That was years ago. Makes sense he'd end up at a place like Tootsies. It's a real goin' concern, ain't it?"

Sonny had insisted on driving himself to Harriman to pick up the CD. He agreed to take his cell phone and the list of questions he and Jenny had made earlier. "I'll take Sixty-one through Oliver Springs, stay off the highway. Nothing to get me upset," he'd told his wife. "I'll even write down Jerry's answers."

So, here he was in Jerry's upstairs office. Sonny had stopped to purchase a six-pack of Heineken and a cheap Styrofoam cooler—he'd not mentioned that to his wife.

While consuming their first round, they exchanged short versions of their life stories. In the early '80s, Jerry had been under contract to

Arista Records in Nashville. He'd tried his hand at songwriting and performing but found that he was better at the production end of the business. Names like Merle Haggard, Willie Nelson and Kenny Rogers fell out of his mouth as if they were long-lost pals. "I got out of the rat race, Sonny," he'd said earlier. "I make more money in the exterminator business than I ever did in Nashville. Ya have to be careful; the record companies'll chew you up and spit ya out!"

At his new friend's insistence, Jerry put on a CD of some of his old recordings. "As you'll hear," he told Sonny, "your stuff is a whole lot better. You might just have a chance, if you know what to watch out for."

"This sounds alright to me." Sonny tapped his foot to the beat. They listened for about half the number. "Did you write this one?" It was a Country train song; as Jerry had admitted, it wasn't very original.

"Yeah, back in the day…" He fingered a remote, there on his desk, to turn off the music. "That's enough of that."

He watched Sonny take a paper from his jeans pocket. "Whatcha got there?"

"I told Jen I'd bring these…questions, write some stuff down." He spied a pen on the desk. "Let me borrow that."

Jerry took a pull on his second Heineken and handed him the pen. "Fire away, Coach."

Sonny reached on the floor beside him to retrieve another beer from the cooler. "I appreciate this, Jerry. Jenny and I know *nothing.*

"Let's start with money. How does someone…you know, how do they get paid? For having a song played on the radio?"

Jerry put his feet up on the desk and rocked back. "Write down BMI and ASCAP, A-S-C-A-P. You join one of those. They do the trackin' and send you a check."

"It's that simple?"

"Almost. Look it up on the Web. They've got links for all their documents and explanations of how they do business." He took a long swallow. "Next question?"

"Okay. Money again, how much do you get paid for doing a…" He searched in the space above Jerry's head for the word he wanted.

"Concert?"

"Yeah, I know the tickets are expensive."

Jerry belched noisily, fooling around. "There, that's better…

"Your songs are Christian—that means you're in the wrong end of the business from the git-go. Christian concert tickets generally run around ten bucks, that doesn't leave a lot to divvy up. At some of 'em they pass the hat—they call it a 'love offerin'. Christian concerts are a hard way to make a livin'."

Sonny laughed at that; then opened his beer. After some thought he observed, "I guess I better pray to…what do you call it, 'crossover'?"

"Yeah, if you could crossover into regular Country; those guys make the big money. What's next on your paper?"

"How much am I gonna have to invest in order to start getting my love offerings?"

The studio manager tapped three fingers on the desk. "Make a list. Three things: promotions, practice, and demos."

Sonny wrote the words, leaving room for Jerry's explanations.

"The record companies sell promotion packages—to let the public know about upcomin' concerts—they get a big chunk of the take."

He paused while Sonny made notes. "Practice sounds simple. But think about that 'Mountaintop' song of yours. It needs a banjo and a fiddle or two to make it work on stage."

"Okay," Sonny said, taking a break for another swallow. He reached in his pocket and beeped once. Noticing his drinking partner's concern…"No sweat, just a little adjustment, I'm fine."

"So," Jerry continued, "you'll probably have to use some house musicians. Not only do they get a cut of the take, but they have to learn your arrangement. Practice time ain't free, either."

"Ungh!" Sonny looked up from his note taking. "What about…demos? We already cut three." He gestured at the CD lying on Jerry's desk. "We've got that covered, right?"

"Maybe." He nodded. "Like I said, the 'Mountaintop' song may need a redo with more backup. Even if the two angel songs are acceptable—which I'd sure say they are—the record company may decide that since you don't have a full album, they'll put your songs on what they call a 'Compilation Disk'."

Sonny wrote 'Comp CD' and looked up.

"That's where the company puts your song on a disk with six or eight other yahoos and sends it off to the radio stations in your market. They charge you for that, too, of course."

Sonny dropped the pen on the desk. "You know, I brought us some beer so we could have a nice, friendly visit…" He laughed. "…about how I was gonna get rich, real quick! You don't get many points for encouragement, Buddy!"

Jerry ignored the 'Buddy'. "Go back to the first thing on your list."

He studied his notes. "BMI?"

Jerry finished his second beer. "Pass me another…

"Okay now, Coach. Let's do a little math. Two hundred radio stations play one of your songs five times a day for a month. What's that?"

"I have no idea." He scratched his neck, self consciously. "Like I told you, Jerry, I'm on dis…disability; I couldn't figure my age divided by the length of my nose."

Jerry put his feet down, grabbed a pencil and doodled on the back of an invoice pad. "Thirty times five is one-fifty. One-fifty times, say twelve cents a play—that's the rate for performin', last I knew. So that's eighteen bucks; times two hundred stations, thirty-six hundred bucks!"

"Wow!"

"Then, you get hot and sell a hundred thousand CD's at nineteen bucks a pop. You're in the big time, boy!"

Sonny clunked his bottle against Jerry's. "I'd like to thank the little people," he murmured. Then: "We're rich, Jerry. I want you as my agent!"

"Trick is, how much of that you get to keep? The recordin' companies are better at math than me and you. They're gonna get their slice and a whole lot more! Don't quit your day job."

Finishing his beer, Sonny slid his question sheet across the desk. "Copy those numbers on here. Jenny will never believe this." He laughed.

Jerry shook his head. "I probably way over-exaggerated, Sonny.

We'd better not get her hopes up too high. Speakin' of your day job, what do you get? Like two-thirds of you teachin' salary, something like that?"

He nodded. "That's about right."

Jerry tossed his empty bottle at Sonny. "Dead soldier…My point is, once you make your first buck singin', you've gone back to work, you're no longer eligible for disability. The money stops. Am I right?"

Sonny put the empty on the floor, beside the cooler. "Rock and a…rock and a…*hard* place, right?" He stood, offering his hand. "This has been…enlightening."

He leaned down to gather his empties and the cooler; then pulled out another bottle instead, opening it and handing it to Jerry. "You get the last two, for disposing of the empties."

Jerry took the bottle. "I get the trash detail, huh?"

Sonny picked up his notepaper and his new demo CD from the desk. "Well, now I know where to come in…Roane County to split a six-pack." He smiled. "Thanks, Jerry. Even if nothing else ever…you know, nothing ever comes of this—I've enjoyed talking with you."

"Anytime," Jerry said, walking him to the door. "I'm here if you need any more CDs cut." He grinned. "Or if ya get the urge to have a couple beers on a Thursday afternoon."

He opened the door. "Holler at Rose on your way out," he called after his new friend, "tell her I'm takin' a nap on the couch."

Chapter 12

After supper, Jenny told Sonny, "Oh, Jerry Hinkle called earlier, I forgot to tell you. He said he had an idea." She smiled at him. "I'll be downstairs; I'm in the middle of cutting out a dress pattern."

Sonny dialed. "Jenny said you called?"

"Yeah," Jerry said, there was mischief in his tone. "I got an idea for y'all. Listen…" He told Sonny his plan.

When his wife came back upstairs, Sonny asked if she had time to look something up on the computer.

"Sure."

They found the U.S. Copyright Office website for the Library of Congress. "Jerry said to look under 'Forms' for 'Sound Recordings'."

They printed the two-page form and a copy of the instructions.

"Good," he said, looking them over. He got up from the daybed and went into the living room, opening the bottom compartment of the end table next to the recliner, pulling out all of his Indian tablets.

Jenny followed along.

"Want to ride with me tomorrow, back to Harriman? It'll take most of the morning—I already looked at the calendar; we don't have Meals." He carried the stack of tablets to the dining table and sat down.

Jenny came to join him. "You had all those out just yesterday. Did you decide to record another song?"

"All of 'em, Jen."

"What?"

"Well, not all of them, really, just the ones…just the ones we think are good enough." He placed his hand on top of the stack of tablets; then stopped. "I need something to write with." He got up to get a red marker from the sofa-table behind the loveseat.

"Alright, here we go." He read from the first tablet. "'247 Pray', remember that one?"

"The one about people dialing a prayer line for help?" She shook her head, trying to figure out where he was going with all this. "Copyright forms and now we're…What *are* we doing, grading songs?"

He nodded.

"Okay, the '247 Pray' song is hokey!"

"Hokey? What are you, a critic? I like that song, it, it tells a story."

Jenny grinned. "Sonny, you like *all* your songs." She shrugged, going along. "Okay, I'll vote it as a keeper." As he put a red check in the corner and lifted to the next page, she touched his hand. "Sonny?"

"Yeah?" He'd been waiting for her interruption.

"What's Jerry's idea?"

He laid the tablet back on the stack. "We printed off the…the copyright forms."

"Yes…"

"And now…" He gestured at the stack. "We're going through all these. Deciding which ones need to be…" He was stuck for the word he needed.

"That's Jerry's idea, to *copyright* all these?" She emphasized his missing word. "That instruction sheet says you have to submit thirty dollars. This could get expensive."

Sonny's smile kept getting bigger. "Nah. You can submit a whole bunch on one form, as many as you can get on a CD, I guess."

"That's my other question," she said, concern in her expression. "Won't it be hard on you, recording a bunch of songs, all in one day?"

He stood up, making a silly theatrical gesture, jabbing his index finger into the air above his head. "Aha! Not so fast, 'Doubting Thomas'!" The movement caused the neurostimulator to zap him. "Ungh!" he grunted, grabbing his neck.

But his smile came right back as he sat down. "Unlike you, my little critic…" He waggled his fingers, doing Groucho Marx. "The Library of Congress doesn't care about the…*quality* of the recordings. I can make a CD of all these songs without ever turning up my controller!

"All they require is a recording—regardless of the quality—and a…"

Jenny shrugged, not able to guess what else was required.

Sonny came up with it, shaking one of them in his hand. "…*song sheets*. All we need are recordings and song sheets."

Jenny was smiling now, seeing the merit of Jerry's idea. "But those are your only copies." She gestured at the stack of Indian pads. "A lot of them are just scratch sheets, with a bunch of cross-outs."

"You can type them for me, can't you, Babe?" His expression was 'Begging Puppy'.

"Don't give me that look," she scolded, but didn't lose her grin. "You're not helpless. We can each do some, using Word, on the computer."

"Oh, I almost forgot…" Sonny said. "Jerry says we have to put your name and address at the bottom of each song sheet."

"Sure, alright, we can make a template."

He tapped her on the wrist. "I said *your* name…on the bottom." He watched her eyes.

He wasn't disappointed, Jenny's face lit up! "*My* name?"

"Yep!" He was laughing aloud now. She was confused. Which meant Jerry's plan was as good as he'd hoped.

She drew back her hand, eyeing him. "*I* didn't write these songs."

"Let me ask you, Jen, who gets…who gets paid for being the author of a song?"

"You…Well, us. We always share, of course. It's always been *our* money, no matter which check it came from."

She put her hand under her chin and sat still for a while, considering. Abruptly her eyes jumped again!

"You got it! Right?" He chuckled.

"Disability…" she murmured. Then she put up her palm, offering a high-five to her husband. "That Jerry is a genius!"

Sonny slapped her hand and grinned some more.

She got up from the table. “I’m going to put some water on for coffee. We’re going to have a long evening—going through all *my* songs.”

Chapter 13

Sonny had a relapse. His body gave him a reminder of his status; he was a disabled individual. For three days he was confined to flat-on-his-back rest in a dark room. He understood what was happening—it had happened every few weeks, once a month or so, for the last two years—his nervous system had endured excess pain for too long; his body was shutting down. The exhaustion brought on alternating bouts of heavy fever and cold sweats.

The neurostimulator provided some sporadic relief, but most of the time it was impossible for Sonny to find a setting that could make the pain tolerable. It made more sense to turn the device off and ride it out. Only rest—long periods of fitful sleep—could restore him.

"He told me to call and tell you. He's one sick puppy!" Jenny told Jim Norton. "He won't be able to make it to that tournament this weekend."

He'll be alright…We've been through this before. Jenny tried to reassure herself. Other than the occasional 'chicken soup' remedy to try to keep him hydrated, there was nothing she could do. She knew he would come out of this in a couple of days, he always had before. But there was always that fear within her: maybe this time his system had endured too much…maybe this time he would not recover!

Don't be paranoid!

But this time her fears were intensified. Would his intentional abuse of the neurostimulator cause this setback to be worse in some way?

Chapter 14

Sonny slept through the night on Sunday. Monday morning he awoke feeling well. "I'm back among the living," he told his wife over the phone.

Jenny was at the hospital, doing her usual Monday morning volunteer work. "Great!" Tears filled her eyes when she heard the energy in his voice. He'd made it! Another bad spell was behind them. She wanted to rush home to hug him and celebrate, but she knew it was better to downplay her elation. She knew in Sonny's mind it was over—his body had failed, but he had recovered—it was time to get on with living. "What's on your agenda for today, Hon?"

"I'm gonna go do the copyright thing with Jerry."

"Need me to drive? I'll be done here by eleven-thirty."

"Nah, I'm alert and ready to go! See you around lunch time."

Sonny recorded a total of 11 songs for copyrighting. Jerry wouldn't hear of payment for the recording time; it was his idea, after all. The session went very smoothly; they took a break in the middle of recording to grab a late breakfast. Admittedly, without using the increased amperage settings from his neurostimulator, the music quality wasn't very good.

When he got back home, he began the task of typing the song sheets. There was no need for chord notations, just simple copying of the lyrics was all that was required, but it turned out to be a task that only Sonny could do. Jenny would never have been able to decipher which Indian tablet sheet contained the final version of the lyrics; versions of the same song might appear on several different tablets. For some songs, the accurate final lyric existed only in Sonny's head.

At the bottom of each song sheet he inserted a template:

Jenny Jacobs
105 Upsal Rd.
Oak Ridge, TN 37830
(865) 425-0543
Sonnyandjen@bellsouth.net

Jenny brought home Petros for lunch. After their chili-and-Frito feast, Sonny finished his typing while Jenny caught up on some bookkeeping for the volunteers.

He tabbed to their email software. There was a correspondence from John Tyler.

From: JohnTyler@tootsies.net
Date: Monday, March 28, 2005, 10:18 AM
To: Sonnyandjen@bellsouth.net
Cc: Joel@joelReed.com,
lynne@SouthernChristian.com
Subject: Re: Saying Howdy

Hi Jenny and Sonny,

Sorry I've been a while following up. Joel gave you a good contact for your music. I've worked on a few projects with Lynne myself. I'll pass along a good word.

Sure enjoyed your songs, Sonny. Or is it Jacob? Lol!

Regards,

John Tyler

"Hey, Jenny!" he yelled into the living room.

"Yes?"

"Come in here. We got another email. This one's from John Tyler."

"Hmm…John says this Lynne person is a good contact," Jenny said, reading over his shoulder.

"You know, we never have called her. You talked to whoever answered the phone to get that price quote, right?"

"Yes, they wanted seventeen hundred dollars for what Jerry did for sixty-five."

"Yeah, I remember. But both Joel and John recommend her. Maybe you should give her a call, at least follow up."

"I guess it couldn't hurt to email her." She bumped his shoulder. "Get up from there and let an expert get to work."

Sonny got up and moved to the edge of the daybed. "Go for it."

"We can find out about some of the other services they offer. I'd like to see what they'd charge to promote an album. Thanks to Jerry, we know a lot more about the music business than we did before."

Sonny nodded. "We sure do."

"Her address is right here." She pointed at the 'Cc' line on the screen. "I can even email her one of the demo songs you recorded with Jerry."

Sonny patted the shoulder of her sweatshirt. "You're becoming quite the little computer student, Ms. Jacobs." He let his hand slide down. "We might be able to come up with a special reward for your hard work."

She giggled but didn't move his hand from her breast.

After a moment he eased away, sitting back down. "I'll give you credit, Jen. You did a good job, using that 'Media Player' software to load those three demos. They sound as good on the computer speakers as they do on our stereo.

"But you don't really know how to email a song, do you?"

Jenny turned to him, beaming. "I sent an attachment of a Dolly Parton song to Rache a couple days ago. She played it on her PC; it worked fine."

"She's got that same software?"

"I guess it's the same. Anyway, it worked alright." She reached for his knee, sliding her hand up along the seam of his jeans. "Now, about that special reward, Coach Jacobs, what did you have in mind?"

****

"Okay, everybody out!" Jenny laughed.

"I'm not through washing the good parts," Sonny called from inside the shower stall. He inadvertently tucked his head, laughing at his reply, "Ouch!"

"Tender?"

Ignoring her question, Sonny pulled the curtain aside and stepped onto the bathmat, reaching for a towel. "You can have it."

As she entered, circling around him…"Get a move on, Jen. I want to watch you send that email."

"I'll be a few minutes. I have more good parts to wash than you, Hon. Go pour me a Pepsi."

****

"Why are you going into Word?" They were back at the computer, Jenny at the keyboard, Sonny watching from beside her. "Aren't you doing an email?"

"I don't know exactly what we want to say," she answered. "I'll type it here then paste it into email after we figure it out."

She typed:

Dear Lynne,
Attached please find a recording of "Angel In The Driveway."

"Jenny!"

She retyped the title and kept going.

Dear Lynne,
Attached please find a recording of "Angel With The Light In His Eyes." This was one of the songs performed by Jacob at Tootsies, on Sunday, March 20th. I believe you have been contacted by Joel Reed and John Tyler about the response the song received.
As the copyrighted author of the song, I am requesting that you evaluate the recording and contact me concerning…
Sincerely,

"How's that?" Jenny asked.

"'Attached please find' sounds stuffy."

"Alright, what else?"

"Make it, 'the *GREAT* response'!" He laughed. "What about the dots at the end?"

She shrugged. "I don't know what we want from her." She paused. "Record? Publish? Distribute? Make a hit record?"

"I vote 'publish'," Sonny answered. "Contact you *how*? By phone or email?"

"I'll send everything, let her choose." She thought another moment. "I'll carbon copy Joel and John on this. Oh, and Toni, too, even thought we've not heard from her."

"Go for it!" Sonny said.

From: Sonnyandjen@bellsouth.net
Date: Monday, March 28, 2005, 2:45 PM
To: lynne@SouthernChristian.com,
Cc: Joel@joelReed.com,
JohnTyler@tootsies.net,
Toniclarkston@Countryconnections.com
Subject: Recording attached
Attach: "Angel With The Light In His Eyes" (WMA file)
"Angel With The Light In His Eyes" (WORD Doc.)

Dear Lynne,

Attached is a recording and song sheet for "Angel With The Light In His Eyes." This was one of the songs performed by Jacob at Tootsies, on Sunday, March 20th. I believe you have been contacted by Joel Reed and John Tyler about the GREAT response the song received.

As the copyrighted author of the song, I am requesting that you evaluate the recording and contact me concerning the possibility of publication.

Jenny Jacobs
105 Upsal Rd.
Oak Ridge, TN 37830
(865) 425-0543
Sonnyandjen@bellsouth.net

“Good work, Babe!” Sonny said. He gestured at the stack of song sheets on the printer. “All we need to do is find a big envelope and go to the post office. Jerry says as soon as it’s mailed, we’re home free as far as the copyright goes.”

Chapter 15

At just after 4:00 PM that same Monday afternoon, the phone rang. Sonny was settling in for a nap on the couch in Jenny's downstairs sewing room. Jenny answered, "Hello?"

"This is Lynne Lewis, with RMG in Nashville. Is this Ms. Jacobs?" The woman sounded young, enthusiastic. Her voice had a melodic quality, as though she were singing her greeting.

Jenny set aside the scissors she was using to cut out a pattern. She nudged her husband's feet to make herself a place to sit. He opened his eyes. "Is that her?"

Jenny nodded and answered her caller, "Yes, this is Jenny. I guess you got my email? Thanks for calling, Ms. Lewis."

"Call me Lynne," she sang. She pronounced her name like singer Leann Rimes: 'Lee-anne'. "Is it alright if I call you 'Jenny'?"

"Sure."

"Well, Jenny!" she gushed, "that song y'all sent me is great! Just great! I played it for Mr. Randall, our publisher, and he just loved it!" 'Mr. Randall' was a question in the middle of her sentence. 'Mr. Randall? publisher?'.

"Glad you liked it..." Jenny stifled the urge to mimic the girl's enunciation. "Lynne."

"I have a question for y'all, right off, Jenny."

"About 'Sonny' and 'Jacob', right?"

"Right, you said 'Jacob' in your note, but Joel said his name is 'Sonny'. Some of our performers use a stage name, so that's fine with me." 'Lee-anne' talked like Reba McEntire sings, stretching words, adding an extra syllable to accommodate the rhythm of her sentences, 'fine' was 'fa-ahn'.

"Whichever we call him, your husband sure can sing, Jenny, and that angel song is fascinatin'!"

Sonny was amused, watching his wife—her eyes twinkled as she struggled to keep from laughing aloud. "Let's do that, Lynne. Use 'Jacob' as his performing name." She winked at her husband.

"Well, that's just fine. Glad we got that little matter cleared up." She paused, checking off notes she'd made ahead of time. "Now, Jenny, you mentioned 'publishin' in your note. Accordin' to John Tyler, Sonny is a great *performer*—really knocked 'em dead at Tootsies! John and I go way back, by the way."

Jenny couldn't help but laugh at the 'way back'. The girl sounded not a day over seventeen. "John mentioned he'd worked with you."

Lynne explained, "My daddy, Larry Lewis, was a studio guitar player for most of the Country acts in Nashville in the sixties and seventies." Again it was a question: 'my daddy? Larry Lewis?'

"I was playin' at Opryland before I was sixteen, backup for some of the groups that did shows at the park." She finally took a breath. "Anyhow, I played some studio gigs for John when he was in the recordin' end of things."

"Long story…" she continued. Jenny could almost see her wave of dismissal. "Turns out, I have a pretty good ear for talent. I've been with RMG for about two years now."

"Well, you're certainly enthusiastic!" Jenny blurted, and then toned down her comment. "I mean, it's good that you've maintained your enthusiasm for your work." She guided the conversation back to its original direction. "You were saying…about Sonny performing?"

She looked at Sonny and shrugged.

"Oh, yes, about John and all. Well, Jenny, RMG provides a number of services." 'Number' and 'services' were multi-syllabic works-of-art off Lynne's tongue. "Judgin' by this recordin' y'all sent me? I would encourage Jacob to let us put together a promotion package for him. He has Star Quality! We'd like to get him to come here, to our studios, and go over some options."

"I'm sure that would be very interesting, Lynne."

Sonny's expression wanted to know what was interesting. She put her palm over the phone. "Star Quality!" she whispered, winking and pointing at Sonny.

Then aloud, "You mentioned your publisher?"

"Mr. Randall?" Lynne answered. "Yes, Mr. Randall is our publisher. And as I said, Mr. Randall has listened to your song and likes it very much…"

Another pause. "I wonder, Jenny, are you acting as Jacob's agent? Is he not wanting to talk to me himself?"

The question was totally unexpected. Over the past couple of years, with his health problems, it had become second nature for Jenny to speak on her husband's behalf. Now this girl was accusing her of…Well, she wasn't sure that Lynne was accusing her of anything.

She and her husband had never talked about it. *Was she Sonny's agent? Did he want to talk to Lynne himself?* Those questions had never entered her mind. She put her hand over the phone again.

Sonny saw the uncertainty in her expression. He had no idea what had transpired. He could hear the woman's voice from the phone earpiece. "Jenny…" the girl was saying. "Ms. Jacobs?"

"Jen, what is it?" Sonny asked.

Her facial appearance changed again…hurt, confused. She took her hand away from the mouthpiece. "Let me call you back," she murmured, then pushed the 'End' button on the phone.

"What's up?" Sonny asked. "Did she say something to upset you?"

Jenny shook her head. "No, I just need a break. I need to think about things for a while, let everything sink in. I'm going to the back porch for a while."

****

Later, at the kitchen table, Sonny laughed at his wife's description of 'Lee-anne's' musical speech pattern. He dismissed her concern about speaking for him. "Far as that goes, Jen, I guess you *should* be my agent. You think better on your feet than I do, since I started having my…pain."

Jenny brought up RMG's interest in him as a performer.

"I thought we were going with, you know, getting the songs published?"

She twisted a strand of hair over her ear and sipped her Pepsi. "That's what I thought. With Jerry's idea about the copyrights…" She was hesitant. "But the girl said you had 'Star Quality', Hon."

Her eyes studied his face, trying to discern his true feelings, as she rushed ahead with her explanation. "At first I thought she was exaggerating, but I'm pretty sure she was serious. I couldn't make that kind of decision, Sonny.

"I mean, there *is* a risk if you perform, we both know that, but I would never try to tell you that you shouldn't."

Sonny smiled. "Star quality. That's pretty good, don't you think? Coming from someone who's…in the business? What is she, a promoter?"

Jenny nodded. "I guess so, she said they had some promotion packages for you to consider."

He hurried to correct her. "Us, Jen, for *us* to consider. That part's already settled. I *do* want you to talk for me, after we decide. What's a pro…"

"Promotional package?" Jenny shook her head. "I have no idea what she meant. But if they want you to *perform*, is that something you'd like to do?"

He laughed uneasily. "Remember the joke about the kid in the vestibule? The priest tells him he'll go blind, looking up into the choir loft, under the girls' dresses?"

"You mean 'I'll squint with one eye until it gets blurry'?" Jenny laughed. "Let's say they wanted you do some sort of show? How many songs do you think you could sing?"

Sonny's expression clouded, recalling Jerry Hinkle's warning. "Wait, I can't make any money, remember? I can't get paid to sing, we already figured that part out."

Jenny got up and carried her glass to the refrigerator for a refill. "You want any more milk?"

"No, thanks."

When she came back to her chair…"Jerry told you sometimes they just pass the hat, play for nothing, didn't he?"

He pulled the controller from his pocket and beeped twice—this was stressful. He put it back and answered, "Yeah, a 'love offering'. Our congregation did that sometimes when college choir groups came to First Christian, remember?" He thought a moment. "Would it help, Babe? Would it help us get our songs pub…published, if I made a couple of 'em popular first?

"You know? Like if I sang at a couple of con…concerts for free?"

Jenny's eyes betrayed her. Sonny was hoping this new idea would meet with her favor. It might be fun to let his Star Quality shine, just for a little while, despite the damage it could do to his health. But his wife's eyes were doing a poor job of disguising her opinion: an emphatic 'No!'

"Listen, Jen…" He pressed the point before she could verbalize her answer. "I'm doing better since I got the neuro…neurostimulator. I have four or five good days before…

"And you'll have to admit, I'm getting better at controlling my temper."

Jenny shook her head, lowering her eyes to the glass in her hand. "I can't stop you, Sonny." She peered up at him. "You already know how I feel. I *like* the fact that you're improving; it's very encouraging. But we both know that making music is dangerous for you.

"But no matter how I feel, *you* have to decide."

She straightened her back and held out her hand. "As your agent, I'm willing to accompany you to this publisher's office. We may as well listen to what they have to offer. Let's shake on it."

He shook her hand, grinning at the mock formality.

"We'll go to Nashville and find out about your Star Quality." She held up her hand. "But…"

Sonny cocked his head. "What?"

"But," Jenny said emphatically, "we won't commit to anything until we discuss the specific 'promotions' they have in mind." She hesitated again. "And…"

"Yeah?"

"And they have to agree *not* to pay you!" She laughed.

Sonny laughed with her. "Oh, speaking of money. How much have we actually spent, so far? We paid sixty-five for the music thing…the *CD* of three songs. And Jerry didn't charge us for the copyright CD. What else?"

Jenny reached for her purse, extracting a folded sheet of paper; she was keeping a detailed list. She showed it to him:

Wal-Mart download	0.94
Custom Sound CD (3)	65.00
Register of copyrights	30.00
Postage	4.81
CD writer	97.12
Recordable CDs (pkg. of 5)	6.05
	203.92

"The sub-total is right at two hundred dollars."

"Do we need to transfer anything from savings?"

"No, this is all on the credit card. I'm keeping receipts so we can keep track. We're still under five hundred, that's what we agreed upon as our budget."

"We're about half that already. They better not want any money for their…what did she call it?"

"Promotion. No, we're not going to give *them* any money. Agreed?"

"I agree."

"Good. And we'll have to scrimp if we go to their office in Nashville, not spend the night or anything.

"We ready to call 'Lee-anne' back?"

"Yeah," Sonny answered, "let me talk to her first, alright?"

"Sure." Jenny hit redial and handed him the phone.

****

When the promoter from RMG came to the phone, Sonny confirmed with Lynne that Jenny would do the talking for them both. "She's better on the phone than I am," he explained, and then handed the phone to his wife.

A quick look at the week's calendar showed Meals assignments for both Wednesday and Friday. "We can come either Thursday or the first of next week," Jenny told Ms. Lewis. They decided on Tuesday, April 5th.

"That will give you time to receive our brochures in the mail and look things over," Lynne told her. "Have y'all seen our website?"

She assured her that they had.

"I need to give you our address, Jenny. RMG is Randall Music Group and our street address is 1201 Division Street."

"We can find that," Jenny said. She asked to be sure Mr. Randall, the publisher, would be available for Tuesday morning's appointment.

"Absolutely, Jenny, he'll sure be here!" Lynne wanted to make one last enthusiastic pitch—it was a competitive business. If John Tyler recommended Jacob and if he was only half as good in person as he sounded on the recording she'd received, this was one she didn't want to get away!

"We're really excited about talkin' with y'all, Jenny! Jacob is a very talented musician; RMG would really like to represent him. Well, both of you, really, of course, since you wrote the songs...Your *song* is great, Jenny, really great!"

"Really..." Jenny mimicked for Sonny after she hung up. "Jacob is *really* talented and your song is great, too, Jenny, *really* great!" She shook her head and rolled her eyes. "Talk about over the top! This should be some meeting."

Chapter 16

They heard from Lynne again, unexpectedly, later that same afternoon. Sonny was just getting out of the shower after his walk. He wrapped a towel around his middle and hustled into the kitchen. "Hello?" His hair was still wet, he wiped at the drops of water trickling down into his eyes.

"Jacob? This is Lynne Lewis again!" Her voice was as enthusiastic and musical as last time. "I'll just bet y'all didn't expect to hear from me again so soon." The 'hear' was 'he-ear', to make her sentence a bright little tune; Sonny couldn't help but laugh.

Before he could say anything, Lynne pressed forward. "Jacob, I have a wonderful surprise for y'all!"

She was breathless. Sonny pictured her jumping up and down like a little kid, tingling with delight. "Are you sittin' down, Jacob?"

"Wait just a minute, Lynne," Sonny knocked on the kitchen window, getting Jenny's attention. She hadn't heard the phone ring—she was loading blackened sunflower seeds into the bird feeder. She looked up when he knocked.

"Hang on," he said again. He opened the kitchen door and held the phone out to his wife. "Le-anne," he told her, sotto voce, grinning. "She has a *wonderful* surprise!"

Jenny stepped around him as he closed the door, taking the receiver. "Lynne?"

"Oh, Jenny, hi! This is Lynne Lewis!" She paused. "Well, you already know that, don't you? Silly me!"

"What's up?" Jenny asked, sitting down. Sonny sat too, crossing his legs in the wet towel.

"Jenny, have y'all ever heard of the Gaylord Entertainment Center?"

Jenny reached to trace a trail of water across the bridge of her husband's nose. "Yes, we've seen it but we didn't go in. It's that green glass cone-shaped building right across the street from Tootsies." Sonny blinked a question; she shrugged, still waiting to hear Lynne's big surprise.

"That's right, Jenny." Lynne was still bubbling. "And of course you've heard of Clifton Jenson."

"Who?"

Ms. Lewis was astounded that Jenny didn't recognize the name. "Clifton Jenson!" she gushed. "Two thousand five's Music Evangelist of the Year! Clifton Jenson!"

Jenny shrugged again at her husband, still waiting for the gist of the message. "Sorry, Lynne," she answered, "I guess we're out of touch, here in the sticks of East Tennessee."

Despite the lack of reciprocal enthusiasm, Lynne was determined to make her wonderful announcement. "We want Jacob to *open* for Clifton Jenson! At Gaylord Entertainment Center!"

It took a long time for the effervescent message to sink in. Jenny was expecting some silly fluff from this bubbly airhead from Nashville. *What was she saying?*

"Jenny, did you hear me?" the music promoter was asking, "Jenny…"

Jenny looked at Sonny; her eyes kept getting wider. He thought she might burst a vessel. "What is it, Babe?"

She still didn't answer. She was mute, unable to speak.

Lynne Lewis was still trying to get through. "Jenny? Jenny?" she kept saying, "Ms. Jacobs, are you there?"

Finally finding her voice…"Yes, we're here. Could you say that again, please, Lynne?" She held the phone out, gesturing for Sonny to listen.

"We want Jacob to open for Clifton Jenson!" Lynne repeated, no less enthusiastic than when she first said it. "At Gaylord Entertainment Center!"

"Wow!" Sonny exclaimed.

"Yeah," Jenny said, "Wow!"

****

It took a while for them to fully comprehend, and then a while longer for Jenny and Lynne to work out all the details. It seemed that Clifton Jenson, Southern Christian Association's Music Evangelist of the Year, was scheduled for a performance this coming Friday evening. But Jeanie Marie Truelove, who was supposed to be his opening act, had had an emergency appendectomy. Mr. Randall had okayed Lynne's spur-of-the-moment replacement, subject to Jacob's signing of a promotional contract.

"We'd have to look at the contract, of course," Jenny answered cautiously. "We've not really talked about any of this yet, Lynne. We haven't even been to your office."

"We need to get y'all over here to Nashville tomorrow, Jenny!"

Sonny was listening in, following what was being said. He wiggled his eyebrows, tomorrow was okay with him.

Jenny gave him a thumbs-up; then responded to Lynne. "This is kinda sudden, but alright. If we leave early we can get there about eleven o'clock," she said. "Will that be alright?"

"Perfect! See y'all tomorrow."

****

"Let's see what we're getting into," Jenny said a few minutes later from in front of the computer terminal. She googled 'Southern Christian Association'.

Their website was touting the eleventh annual Southern Christian Music Awards show and encouraging membership in the association. There was also a 'News & Events' link to an article titled: 'SCA gives wings to positive music.' "This is interesting," she noted.

Sonny read over her shoulder. "Hey, the founder of SCA, the Southern Christian Association, is Leroy Randall. Isn't that one of the muc…mucky-mucks at RMG?"

"Yes, that's what I was saying." Reading further, Jenny added, "Four hundred members, their awards show is carried by GAC, that's the Great American Country network. They show videos, like MTV. There's a CMT, too, Country Music Television."

Sonny sat back on the daybed. "So Leroy Randall of…Randall Music Group, the company Lynne works for, is the founder of this association. Small world…"

Jenny clicked on a link within the SCA website, labeled 'Southern Christian Magazine'. She had noticed the reference to Southern Christian in Lynne's email address. It was all starting to make sense.

After a short study of the site…"And guess who the publisher of this magazine is?"

Sonny nodded his head. "Mr. Randall, I'll bet."

"Right." She turned to offer a wary smile. "That world keeps getting a little smaller, doesn't it?"

She had another idea. "Sonny, you remember the 'Dove awards'?"

"Yeah, we watched that show on the tube. Amy…Amy what's-her-name was the only Gospel singer I'd ever heard of. What's her name?"

"Amy Grant."

"Right, Amy Grant…"

Googling 'Dove' led Jenny to a site for 'The 36th annual Gospel Music Association Awards'. "Look at this."

He leaned forward again as Jenny deciphered what she was reading. "Look, the national networks carry the Dove awards show. See: ABC this year…"

"Click the 'membership' link."

She did.

"Well," Sonny read, "that's interesting."

Jenny made the connection with him. "The GMA has four *thousand* members, and SCA has four *hundred*. And the Doves are carried on one of the major networks, not just that Country music channel. They're the big players."

She googled 'GAC' next, the cable network that carried the SCA awards show. "Toni mentioned GAC the other night, remember?"

"No." He shook his head. "But go ahead."

"Toni said something like 'she'd be seeing you on GAC'. Surely Randall doesn't have anything to do with them!"

On GAC's site she found a link for 'Our Management'.

"Nope, at least *they're* not run by Randall. He's not one of their officers or anything; it says their corporate offices are in Centennial, Colorado. I guess Leroy just worked a deal with them to cover his awards show."

Sonny stood up and stretched, tired from all their sleuthing. "Did you put Jerry's number in our address book?" When his wife nodded, he went to retrieve it.

He turned on his cell phone when he came back into the room, their beat-up leather address book in hand. "I should probably put him in my phone listing…" He dialed. "Hi, Rose, is Jerry handy?"

In a moment his new friend was on the line.

"Hey, Jerry, howya doing? Listen, I got some big news, I think. But first I have a question. Have you heard of RMG?"

"Been around 'bout ten years," Jerry answered. "Kind of a one-man outfit, Leroy Randall is tryin' to take advantage of the Country church market. The Dove Awards got kinda far out with all their new *kid* bands, so Randall stepped in with a more conservative approach to Christian Country music."

"So, they're legit?"

Jerry laughed. "Kinda, sorta. You remember I was telling you how the record companies find a way to make most of the money?"

"Yeah?"

"Well, this ol' boy gets 'em comin' and goin'; signs new acts to a ten-K 'promotion' contract and gets his money up front. I think some of his major acts are making some money, though, the ones with videos on the cable networks. What's your big news?"

"Ever hear of Clifton Jenson?"

"Nope."

Sonny made an aside to Jenny, no need to lower his voice or cover the receiver. "He's never heard of him."

Jenny grinned, not surprised.

Sonny went ahead with his news. "That guy we met at Tootsies, Joel Reed, told us to contact RMG, so we did. Jenny emailed them one of my angel songs, wanting to see if they'd consider pub…pub…"

"Publishing?" Jerry prompted.

"Yeah, publishing. A go-getter named Leanne called us, all fired up about me 'opening' for this guy…this *Clifton* guy.

"Anyway…" Sonny was exasperated at his communication impairment! He took a deep breath. "They want me to sing at the Gaylord Entertainment Center."

"Big place," Jerry grunted, "holds about five thousand folks. I thought you'd decided against performin'? Wasn't that why we made those copyrights recordings?"

Sonny's ears reddened. Jenny's face made a question. He blurted out his answer to Jerry. "Well, we thought maybe if I did a couple of shows—if I'm good enough—that maybe Jen would have more luck selling our songs."

Sonny waited for a response but Jerry didn't answer.

"So, what do you think?"

Still no answer.

Sonny took another deep breath; his neck and shoulders were starting to pound. He took a moment to beep twice to adjust for the stress.

"Come on, Jerry," he finally said, "I called because I need your advice."

"Not *my* decision." The answer was flat, noncommittal.

After another pause…"Stick your hand in a basket of snakes and you'll get bit. Randall will want five thousand, at least, before you ever set foot on that stage."

It wasn't what Sonny wanted to hear, but he was thankful for the forthright advice. He tried to brighten his voice. "Listen, Jerry, I appreciate this."

Jenny reached to touch his hand before he hung up. "Ask him if we should…"

Sonny rubbed his neck and handed the phone to her.

"Jerry, this is Jenny…One last question, should we consider them for *publishing* our songs?"

This time Jerry's tone was lighter. Jenny held the receiver so that Sonny could hear his response. "Well, they've got a whole stable of signed artists. They're probably lookin' for songs. Randall'll try to sign y'all to an exclusive demo deal, though."

"We've got an exclusive demo deal with Custom Sound, Jerry," Jenny assured him. She winked at Sonny to encourage him.

Sonny took the phone back, still rubbing his neck. "We're not going away from our agreement with you, Jerry. If they want any demos cut, we get them from you."

"Good luck with that!" Jerry sniggered. But he *did* want to be encouraging. "Go talk to 'em, Sonny. If you can get Randall to go along, you're slicker than most of the acts out there."

He laughed outright. "You *do* have one thing goin' for ya."

"What's that?"

"Your wife!" He raised his voice to make sure Jenny heard him. "Watch 'em Jenny! Make 'em sweat. You've got good songs; they *need* good songs. Go for it!"

"Thanks, Jerry!" they both called into the phone.

"You bet," Jerry said; then hung up.

One more thing occurred to Jenny. She found the website for Gaylord Entertainment Center. Sure enough, Jeanie Marie Truelove was scheduled to be the opening act for Clifton Jenson on Friday night.

"At least Lynne is shooting straight about that," Sonny said.

Chapter 17

"Much ado about nothing." Sonny had stirred a bit; Jenny turned off the stereo hoping he'd sit up and talk with her.

"What?" he asked. He was sprawled in the passenger seat of their Crown Vic, on the return trip from Nashville; they were passing through Crossville. "We didn't accomplish much, huh?"

Jenny looked over at him. "It was like Jerry warned us, they just wanted our money."

"And you weren't giving a penny!" Sonny laughed. "Jerry was right about you, Babe, I'm glad you're on my side."

He adjusted the seat upright, ready to talk now that he'd rested a while. "That 'Lee-anne' is nothing at all like she sounds over the phone. Business suit, nice office, she's what, early thirties?"

Randall Music Group had a large suite of offices and sound studios on the third floor of a red brick building, right on Music Row. Showing them around, Lynne came across as mature and graceful; the thin blonde seemed both confident and competent.

"You can never be too thin or too rich," Jenny had whispered to Sonny when they entered her office.

Leroy Randall was a short guy with thinning, obviously-dyed, black hair that he combed straight back. 'Suave' was the term that came to Jenny's mind when they sat down to converse—Sonny thought he looked like a snake oil salesman.

Jenny was paying attention to a semi coming alongside. She was wearing charcoal wool slacks and a Navy V-neck sweater over a white button-down; her hair was up in her bookkeeper bun for the meeting.

For the meeting, Sonny had worn his usual: running shoes, jeans, blue long-sleeved shirt with a pocket for his controller, and his 'OR' ball cap. When Lynne asked what he would wear to perform he pushed his cap back and gave her the 'Aw Shucks' grin. "This is it." He winked. "I'm not into the cowboy look."

Lynne and Randall had exchanged glances but made no comment. Jenny supposed they'd work on Jacob's RMG-approved 'look' after they got him signed.

When the truck cleared, she answered Sonny's question about Lynne's age, "About that, I'd say, maybe late thirties. You know, once you get by her voice, she seems pretty competent. She had all the facts and figures about Jenson and their other artists. That was an interesting bio on Janey Stallone, the songwriter; from her picture, she looked to be about our age."

"Maybe that'll be you next year, Jen, Songwriter of the Year."

Jenny shook her head. "Not if Mr. Randall has anything to say about it."

Sonny beeped his controller down a notch. "How many times did he say, 'Please, call me Leroy'?"

Jenny grinned, her eyes on the road.

"You kept calling him 'Mr. Randall' and turning down every attempt he made to get us to sign on the dotted line. It was like Jerry told us. Money for promotions, money for their 'media press release' kit to track radio plays, money for demos. Nine hundred bucks for a single song release and what he called 'pitching' our songs. Like he couldn't call one of his string of performers, any time he wanted to, and tell them to come in and record one of our songs."

Jenny sighed. "I tried to talk to him about you singing for free. He was adamant about a contract, though."

"Lynne seemed to get into *that* a little, after he left the office. Singing for free, I mean.

"When you were telling her about my disability? She looked at me the same way everybody does, like: 'Hey, you look alright to me.'" He shuddered, shaking away the creepy feeling of being the object of scrutiny. "Anyway, Lynne seemed interested when you explained your idea about me singing for free because of my disability payments."

"I wonder?"

Sonny touched her hair, using his fingers to massage the back of her neck as she drove. "You wonder what?"

"Ah, that feels nice." She relaxed a minute before answering. She glanced over at him. "Jenson's opening act, whatever her name was. We looked that up on the Gaylord website—that was legitimate; she really *was* scheduled. And did you notice? Lynne mentioned that several times, when Randall was in her office, about them needing an opening act."

"They have dozens of singers, Jen. They should be able to call someone."

She scratched her jaw, thinking about it. "They're not *that* big, you know? As much of a money-grubber as Randall is, they probably keep everybody booked pretty tight. I don't think Lynne wanted to let us out of there without getting you signed.

"She said 'We may still be back in touch', remember, as we were putting on our coats? I wonder if she's in a tight spot? It's probably her responsibility to see that contracts are met; her job could be on the line."

They rode awhile in silence.

Sonny reached into the glove box and found a small yellow pad. There was a pen, too. He started making a list, pausing to chew on the end of the pen as he struggled to add entries.

After a few minutes, curiosity got the best of his wife. "So?"

"I'm making a list. If she *does* call us, she said an opening act did four or five songs. What songs would I do? I'm trying to make a list of songs that might go together."

"What's wrong with the songs you did at Tootsies?"

He touched the point of his pen to items on his list. "I've got 'Angel With The Light In Eyes' as number two and 'Bev's Song' as number four. But I was thinking about 'It's Me Again, Lord' as the first song.

That way, I could just start singing without having to say anything. I'd just start out with:

It's me again, Lord, praying for a friend...

"What do you think?"

Jenny was distracted a moment, thinking back:

Sonny's very first song had been "It's Me Again, Lord." Not long after his cancer surgery, the head nurse at the doctor's office had called to see if Sonny would be willing to visit a man who was facing a *similar surgery. "Wilfred needs some encouragement," the nurse had told him. They visited and Sonny found that encouraging Wilfred wasn't much different from motivating his ballplayers—he was a natural.*

Wilfred's surgery wasn't quite as successful as his new friend's; he had some problems with aspiration and was stricken with pneumonia. Out of the blue, Sonny wrote a song. He carried along his guitar and played the song for Wilfred when he visited him in the hospital. Sonny's friendship and his song were a very real reinforcement for Wilfred, his condition improved. After Wilfred's recovery, his wife Lillian insisted that Sonny perform the song for their church congregation in Lenoir City. That was the start of Sonny's music writing and performing.

"Earth to Jen..." Sonny said, interrupting her reverie.

Jenny shook her head. "I was just thinking about Wilfred, you remember?"

"Of course," he sighed, "it was my first song. I wonder how old Wilfred's doing these days."

He clicked his pen. "Back to the business at hand, Jen."

She smiled. "Right, I'm with you: Wilfred's song, then the first angel song. You could do 'We Will Pray For You' as the third song. Two prayers, two angels, I like it!"

"Okay, so that's four. How about..."

Jenny's cell rang, interrupting Sonny.

Jenny swerved slightly at the sound; she was always surprised when the phone rang while they were traveling. She fished it out of her purse, there beside her, next to the door. “Hello?”

It was Lynne; her tone was more straightforward now that they had met in person, a little less bubbly. “How far down the road are you?” she asked after identifying herself.

Jenny made her wait a half-beat. “We’re a little more than half way home. Why do you ask?”

“Lynne…” she mouthed to Sonny.

Lynne’s tone was that of a conspirator. “I made one final pass at Leroy, Jenny.”

Jenny was purposely short with her. “About…”

Lynne gave Jenny a careless laugh, trying to draw her into the conspiracy. “I think if y’all would turn around and come back for a studio session, we could work this out. Mr. Randall says I have to preview a demo of the songs Jacob would sing, opening for Clifton Friday night.”

Jenny had to give her credit for persistence. “We’ve already talked about that, Lynne. It’s not open to negotiation—Custom Sound is our demo studio.”

Leroy Randall had visibly flinched when Jenny had mentioned Jerry Hinkle at their meeting; clearly their paths had crossed before.

Lynne made a half-hearted effort at returning to fluffy airhead mode. “Well, Jenny, y’all have sure got me in a hard place here.” ‘Hard’ was stretched to ‘ha-ard’ to accommodate the rhythm of her talking. “I even got Mr. Randall to agree to a single performance contract with Jacob, just for this one show.”

Jenny shook her head, smiling at Sonny. “As I told you, Sonny isn’t in a position to accept any compensation.”

Ms. Lewis had a quick reply. “Oh, well, we could make it a ‘services’ contract to *you* Jenny, as Jacob’s representative.”

That might be interesting, Jenny thought. “We have fax software as part of our email package. Why don’t you fax me that contract? Call first, so we know to turn on the computer.

“But we’re not going to turn around and come back today, Lynne, under any circumstance. We'd be worn out, just driving back and forth."

She gave some thought to Lynne's requirement to preview Sonny's songs. "We could go by Custom Sound tomorrow morning, Wednesday, and record the other songs for you to review. Is five songs enough?"

Now it was Lynne's turn to pause. Jenny could picture her, drumming her fingers on her fancy hardwood desk. "Five songs would do fine, Jenny, assuming we can work all this out." 'Fine' came out 'Fa-ahn' again. "Listen, I'll have to get back to you on all this." Lynne tried to brighten her tone as she rang off. "You and Jacob have a good trip home, ya hear. We'll be talkin' again, real soon."

"How'd she get your cell number?" Sonny wanted to know as she put the phone back in her purse.

"It was on that form I filled out when we first got there." She grimaced, remembering some of the questions. "They wanted stuff like what bank we use and our Social Security numbers. I left all that private information blank."

She passed a slow-moving panel truck, loaded with ladders and swinging PVC pipe. "So, she *did* call us."

"Yeah, you didn't give an inch…told her we were sticking with Jerry." Tapping the pen on his list again, Sonny remembered his idea for the fifth song. "How about 'Rainbows To Paint' for the last song?"

Jenny thought a moment, recalling the lyrics. She recited:

I know my life was changed
by a man with an old guitar,
I'll never be the same…

"That would be perfect, Hon!" It would leave a good parting image, wouldn't it? What does he say? Oh, I remember:

Son, I must be goin', I've got rainbows to paint.

"I like it Sonny. I like it a lot!" She smiled at him. "Now, if Lynne can get Randall to go for it."

****

Lynne called to give them the go-ahead shortly after they arrived at home Tuesday evening. “Send me copies of the songs as soon as you get them recorded.”

Rose, Jerry’s secretary, informed them he’d be busy servicing his exterminator clients all day Wednesday. They would have to wait until Thursday.

Chapter 18

Wednesday morning, Jenny called to ask Brenda, the kitchen supervisor at Meals On Wheels, if she would find a substitute for Friday's assignment. "We may be going out of town," she told her.

Sonny was reflective at lunch. "Jen, you remember when I stopped writing songs before? I told you the Lord hadn't sent anyone to encourage us?"

She sipped a spoonful of her tomato soup. "I remember."

"Well, I don't guess I can say that anymore, can I? I mean, Doug and them listening to our songs, people praying for me to get better."

She took his hand. "You know what? You're right, they never let us down, even when we stopped going."

"And this new guy, Jerry—he's sure been a Godsend, don't you think?"

"I guess you could call him that." She thought a moment, then…"Absolutely! Jerry has really come through for us and we hardly even know him."

"Joel and Toni have been encouraging, too," she added.

Jenny spent the afternoon working on a quilt for the hospital volunteers' rummage sale; Sonny took a first-of-spring swipe at the yard after tuning up the lawn mower.

Later, Sonny called Doug Henson at his office. "Hey, you going to the evening service tonight?"

"I guess," Doug answered. "Why, you got something else in mind?"

"No, I thought I'd get you to pick me up. It's been a while since I've seen some of the guys in men's group. I thought I'd go with you and thank some people for their prayers.

"Besides," he added, "there's lot's of stuff happening in our life right now. It wouldn't hurt to get back into, you know…"

"Sure, I'll pick you up about six-fifteen," Doug told him.

Jenny overheard the conversation. "That's a surprise."

Sonny shrugged.

"Maybe I'll change my clothes and go with you," his wife said.

Chapter 19

Jerry Hinkle was able to fit Sonny in Thursday morning, ahead of a Knoxville gospel group. The two angel songs had already been recorded as demos, there were only three songs to record, but "Rainbows To Paint" was a struggle. Sonny kept changing his mind about the lyrics for the final chorus.

He sang the song the way he'd written it, the version that they'd sent to the copyright office, getting all the way to the last three lines of the song then stopped abruptly.

With every word he sang that night, my life was surely changed
By a man with an old guitar, I'll never be the same
When he said: Son, I must goin', I've got rainbows to paint

"Problem?" Jerry asked, over the communication mic.

"Lyric doesn't sound right…let me work on it minute."

Sonny came out of the sound room and found a pencil and pad on the counter in Jerry's control area. He jotted and crossed out, humming to himself.

Jenny sat where she was, there on the long couch. There was nothing she could do to help his creative process.

"Okay," he finally said, looking at his three new lines, planting them in his memory, "all set."

"From the top on this one?" Jerry asked.

"Yeah." Sonny sang and played the entire song again; three full verses and into the final chorus.

I didn't believe in angels, but I—-

"Crap!" Sonny said. He grasped his guitar by its neck and let it drop to the floor. Angrily, he exited the recording room and kept walking. He opened the studio door and stormed out!

Despite the plush carpeting on the steps, Jenny could hear him clomping down the stairwell.

Jerry pulled his earphones off and looked at her as they heard the lower door close.

"Let him go." She sighed. "There's no reasoning with him until he calms down."

More than ten minutes elapsed before Sonny finally came back into the studio. "Had to blow off some steam," he muttered. His face was red and his neck was throbbing. He reached into his shirt pocket and beeped twice on his controller, glancing at his shoulders to track the stimulation. "That's a little better..."

He looked at the paper with his new song lines and then up at the ceiling, raising his palms in the air for both of them to see. "Forgot the second line. I just wrote this, you'd think I could remember."

He gestured to his wife. "Come in with me, would you?" He tore the piece of paper from the pad and handed it to her. "Hold it up for me when I nod."

She followed him into the studio. With Jenny's help, Sonny got all the way through the song this time, including the final chorus.

I didn't believe in angels, but I know my life was changed
By a man with an old guitar, I'll never be the same
When he said: Son, I must goin', I've got rainbows to paint...

They paid Jerry $130.00 for the recording time. Jerry was his old self; complementary of Sonny's music and wishing them well Friday night. If he was upset or concerned about Sonny performing, he kept it to himself.

****

Lynne enthusiastically approved all five songs after receiving them via email. Jenny had 'Cc'ed' the attachments to John Tyler, Joel Reed and Toni Clarkston, as before.

"Jacob is gonna be a big hit!" Lynne exclaimed when she called back. She faxed a contract for $100.00 to Jenny. 'For transportation and personal services rendered at Gaylord Entertainment Center, Friday, April 1st.'

Jenny called her back. "I thought I'd explained all this, Lynne. Sonny is on disability, there is no way we can accept any compensation for his performing."

Lynne was defensive. "You agreed to a services contract last time we talked. You asked me to fax it to you."

Jenny let out a long audible breath, wanting the music promoter to hear her exasperation. "How many ways can I say this, Lynne? If RMG wants to compensate me for publishing my copyrighted songs, I am willing to talk about money. But we're not going to jeopardize my husband's disability compensation for a trip to Gaylord Entertainment or anywhere else. Your *services* contract, paying me, is totally transparent.

"I thought you meant something like a release…don't you have some sort of liability form?" Jenny was familiar with subcontractor release forms from her days at the DOE plant—the forms limited liability, allowing subcontractors access to the government site.

Lynne's reply was abrupt. "If you'd be kind enough to turn on your fax machine, I'll forward a different form."

This time the release form was acceptable. No money was to change hands and RMG was released from any liability for accidents or injury for the April 1st Gaylord performance only. Jenny signed it and faxed it back.

****

"April Fool's Day," Sonny remarked, at supper Thursday evening when Jenny told him about Lynne's continuing attempts to pay them. He had gone straight to bed after returning from recording. "I hope it's not us who get fooled."

Jenny laughed at his comment but turned her head away as she ate. She was worried.

It had happened again; after the stress of recording at Jerry's, with the amperage turned up, Sonny was manic on the ride home. He kept adjusting his controller, groaning at the intensity of his pain. He was bedridden the rest of the afternoon, another downswing in his health. Friday evening, tomorrow, would *not* be a good time for Sonny to be feeling poorly.

****

That evening she called Rachel. "What's up, Jen?" her friend asked.

"What're you doing tomorrow evening?" She was folding clothes as she talked, balancing the phone with her chin.

"I can't hear you. What are you doing?"

She finished folding a T-shirt and took the phone in her hand. "Sorry, I was trying to fold clothes and talk at the same time. All this running back and forth to Nashville and Harriman has got me behind on my housework," she replied. "I asked what you and Doug are doing tomorrow night."

"I'm not sure, I'll have to check. April Fool's Day is always circled on our social calendar. There're all those green beer parties with the funny Irish hats." She giggled. "No, wait, that's St. Patrick's.

"I haven't been to the video store yet, so I guess we're free, why?"

"Rache…" Jenny paused for dramatic effect. "Are you ready for this?"

"What? Tell me."

"Sonny is going to sing at the Gaylord Entertainment Center."

"Where?"

Jenny sighed. "That big cone-shaped building in Nashville, Rache. It's a huge auditorium. They say it holds about five thousand people."

"And Sonny's gonna sing there? When did all this happen? You've been holding out on me!"

They visited a while.

Sonny had asked Jenny to call Jim Norton, too. With a group of Sonny's fellow teachers, people that Jenny used to work with, and folks from First Christian church, there would be a convoy of four or five carloads following them to Music City.

Chapter 20

Having taken an Excedrin PM Thursday night, Sonny slept late Friday morning. His neurostimulator was turned on through the night, at a setting of 3.0. Before opening his eyes, he took inventory: no gnawing pain, just the usual tightness; he didn't feel nauseous, no headache. *This might work out to be a pretty good day.*

He opened his eyes to look at the clock. 11:04 AM. Well, he'd gotten plenty of rest.

"I thought I'd be awake all night, thinking about the…my singing tonight," he told Jenny as he placed the teakettle on the burner. His wife had heard him stirring and had come upstairs to see how he was doing—he looked well rested. "But I slept like a baby," he told her.

"You had a fever," she said. "The sheets were soaking wet when I came to bed after Letterman. I guess you sweated it all out.

"Are you excited, about tonight?"

He laid out his donuts, blood pressure pill and orange juice while the water heated and sat down to look at her. "I don't think I'm nervous. I know I'll be in another world once I turn the stimulator up, so it won't matter how I feel…before. We have to be there at six-fifteen, right?"

She nodded, getting up to make his instant coffee. She poured herself a Pepsi, too, as he finished his OJ.

Sonny rubbed his hand on the top of his head. "I should probably get you to buzz this before we go. I'm getting fuzzy."

"You'll have your cap on." She grinned. "Anyway, you look fine to me."

"Maybe I'll be able to afford a more co…cooperative barber if we sell some of our songs."

"Hurry and finish your breakfast if I'm going to cut your hair; we'll need to leave about twelve-thirty or one. The last thing we want is to get stuck in traffic.

"You can rest some more in the car, if you want. Save up your energy for tonight."

Sonny nodded at his coffee. "Thanks. Yeah, I think I will rest some. I feel fine, but this will be two days in a row…I know that concerns you."

He gave her a serious look. "It does me, too. I wouldn't do this, Babe, if I didn't think it would really help us get our music pub…published."

Jenny laughed aloud. "Sonny, this is me you're talking to. Save the 'Aw Shucks' for your fans. I know you're as excited about this as I am! Just think, Hon, a couple weeks ago we were thinking about doing a song for the youth group at church. Now you're doing five songs at the Gaylord Entertainment Center!"

****

They pulled in next to where Lynne was standing, beside a black Lincoln Towne Car in the parking lot, up near the rear door of the Gaylord Center. Lynne had asked Jenny to call her cell once they were in Nashville. It was 5:30 PM; they were well ahead of schedule.

Lynne wrinkled her nose at Sonny's appearance as she handed them lanyards with backstage badges. "So, you were serious? This is what you're wearing tonight?"

From running shoes to ball cap, Sonny was dressed for comfort. He was wearing the same blue button-down Oxford-cloth shirt that he'd worn to Tootsies. "My lucky shirt." He winked, slipping on his jacket from the back seat. "Don't worry," he assured her, gathering his guitar case from the trunk, "it's all about the music."

She shrugged, deciding not to agonize over things she couldn't do anything about. She turned to Jenny. "You look very nice."

"Thanks." Jenny was dressed in tan, neatly creased wool slacks with a black silk blouse and a heavy gold-chain necklace. Sonny had asked her to let her hair down; it was brushed out, full and flowing, curls gathering around her gold-hoop earrings.

Doug and Rachel, Karen and Jim piled out of a car that pulled up next to them, Jim's green Explorer. This early, there were very few other cars in the lot. Jenny made the introductions to Lynne.

More friends were exiting from their cars. "Jack stopped to wait on Todd and them at an Exxon, he was about out of gas," explained Marcia Templeton, one of Jenny's former coworkers, as they walked to where the others were standing. "They'll be along in a couple of minutes."

"The ticket office is right around the corner." Lynne pointed to the west. "Y'all will want to stay for Clifton Jenson's show after Jacob performs," she told them—ever the promoter. "Clifton is Southern Christian Association's Music Evangelist of the Year!"

Jim Norton motioned with his chin, around the corner, back east, the way they'd driven in. "Hey, Lynne?"

"Yes?"

"We couldn't help but notice, when we pulled in, the marquee only says—what's his name, 'Clifton Jenson'. Don't they usually put a 'with' for the opening act? Like: 'with Jacob', something like that?"

Lynne put up her hand in a stop sign, wiggling her fingers as if warding off any responsibility. "This has all happened rather quickly. There really wasn't time to give notice to the facilities manager." Realizing the weakness of her reply, she reached to take Sonny's arm. "I'm sure Jacob understands."

Stepping between Lynne and Sonny, Jenny elbowed her aside—her husband didn't need any touchy-feelies from the skinny blonde.

"Listen," she told the gathering group of friends as Jack and Todd's cars were pulling into the parking lot, "we're gonna go on in. Save us a seat and we'll come back and sit with you guys after Sonny's part of the show. We'll all go out for coffee after."

Lynne shrugged off the affront of Jenny's elbowing. "This way," she said, turning on her heel and walking toward the rear entrance of the auditorium.

****

Clifton Jenson had the look: strong block chin, red button-down shirt, open at the collar, and a big white cowboy hat. He was in his early thirties, a down-to-earth guy—cordial. "I really appreciate your filling in for Jeanie Marie, Jacob," he said in a strong baritone, shaking Sonny's hand.

"It's Sonny," he informed the singer, "Sonny Jacobs. I guess you'd say 'Jacob' is my per…performing name."

"Well, nice to meet you, Sonny. Lynne tells me you've got some really great songs!" He introduced the members of his band and offered to show them around. Sonny noticed the guys in the band paid more attention to introductions to Jenny than to him, but he was used to that—all part of being married to an attractive woman.

Clifton gestured at Sonny's ball cap. "O R?"

"Oak Ridge," he answered, "about twenty miles north of Knoxville. Where are you from?"

Clifton's voice reminded Sonny of Porter Waggoner, back in the early television days. "I've been in Nashville for a little over six years now."

Lynne took over, cutting their conversation short. She showed Sonny where he would enter the stage and pointed out the single stool and microphone just in front of the bandstand. "We'll have Clifton's band equipment set up behind you, here." She pointed. "That way, there's no delay after you do your set. There's an open jack, there on the floor. It won't give any feedback when you plug in."

Sonny looked at Jenny, confused.

Jenny understood the look. "Sonny's guitar is acoustic, Lynne. He's got one of those little microphone clip-ons."

Sonny nodded. "That's right. I used it for all my recordings at Cus…Custom Sound. I'd expect your sound guys can pick it up."

Lynne excused herself to make sure Jacob's expectations were correct.

In a few minutes she was back, introducing them to the tubby Master of Ceremonies, Steve Jenkins. "Anything special you need for your intro, Jacob?" he asked in his Ralph Emory voice.

"Nah, nothing special," Sonny answered.

"We've got a pretty good crowd coming," Steve told Lynne. "Looks like a little under four thousand, not counting walk-ins."

"Great!" Lynne gushed.

Jenny supposed gushing was the modus operandi for pre-concert conversation. Lynne had ended every sentence with an exclamation point since they'd entered the theater.

Lynne guided Sonny and Jenny to an island of five large leather lounge chairs in an alcove to the right of the stage. The couple was left alone, calm-before-the-storm, after Lynne was sure everything was squared away. She assured Jenny she'd come and find her a good seat out front, just before show time.

With about 15 minutes to go, John Tyler appeared, walking down a long hall to their right. "Hey, Buddy! Howya doin'?" he asked, putting his hand out for Sonny to shake. He had a guitar case in his left hand.

Jenny and Sonny both rose to greet him. Jenny pushed his hand away and insisted on a hug. "It's so good of you to come, John. We really appreciate the nice things you had to say about Sonny in your emails. I'm sure we wouldn't be here without your recommendation."

John smiled, giving her a wink as they separated. "I think the crowd would rather look at you than listen to your husband, truth be told," he teased, handing the guitar case to Sonny. "Mr. Stratocaster at your disposal, Sonny, knock 'em dead!"

Sonny was floored by the gesture of friendship; he had to sit down, holding the case in his lap. "John, I don't know what to say."

John waved his hand. "No big deal. I thought you'd like to have a *real* instrument if you're gonna try your hand at the Big Time."

"Oh, you know what? I still have that elec…electronic pickup you let me borrow. I used it to make some CDs; I was pla…planning on using it this evening," Sonny said. "You want it back?"

"You can keep it. I've got plenty of those, they're cheap."

He looked at his watch. "Listen, Buddy, I can't stay. We've got a pretty good crowd across the street—Toni and her band are in the front room—I gotta get back."

Jenny reached for another hug before he left. She gestured at the guitar Sonny was unpacking from its case. "We'll get it back to you as soon as we can, John. This was so thoughtful of you."

"I've got a little riding on this, too," he told her, gesturing at Sonny. "I want him to do great!"

He nodded at Sonny, who was still seated; he had the guitar out of its case, running through some chords to make sure everything felt right. "I imagine you'll be doing several more shows before it's all over, you just keep hold of that Stratocaster until you can afford one of your own. I got no use for it myself."

He turned to leave; then remembered something else. "Oh, tell Jerry Hinkle I said 'Hey!'" He laughed. "Jerry called me and we had a good talk about you two."

His eyes narrowed, taking Sonny fully into his gaze. "You be careful, now. A couple good shows and people will be clamoring to record your stuff—then you can let someone else do the singing."

He looked at Jenny. "Good luck with *your* music!" He laughed again. "That Jerry is no dummy!

"I'm out the door," he said over his shoulder as he walked away.

"Thanks again!" Sonny and Jenny called after him.

****

Lynne noticed the Stratocaster right away. She hurried off to let the control room know that Jacob would be using the floor jack after all. Then she came back to escort Jenny to a seat out front. "Break a leg, as they say!" she told Sonny.

Jenny took his chin in her hands and looked into his eyes. "Be careful, Sonny, nothing is as important as your health. Not even your music. I want you to promise me something."

He didn't wait for her to ask. "If I start hurting, I'll stop," he assured her, "even if it's right in the middle of all this." He waved broadly, taking in their strange surroundings. Then he pushed his cap back and gave her his counterfeit 'Aw Shucks' smile. "You go watch. I'll make you proud."

As the two women walked away, Sonny tugged the security-pass lanyard from around his neck, laying it in the nearest chair, on top of his guitar case. John Tyler's Fender guitar case was lying open; he shut it and slid it under his own older case, hoping no one would bother it.

He pulled the neurostimulator from his pocket and upped it eight notches. Within seconds he felt the familiar surge, clear to the fingertips of both hands. The tingling sensation in his forearms was strong. He picked up the Stratocaster and made his way to the wings of the stage.

Chapter 21

The curtain was open; Sonny could see the first few rows of the audience. There was some murmuring, but they were mostly waiting—waiting for the opening act before the big show. "Ladies and Gentlemen…" He heard Steve's voice from somewhere inside one of the huge amplifiers. "Ladies and Gentlemen: Jacob."

Sonny walked slowly and confidently—his posture maybe a little stiff, his expression maybe a bit grim—to pick up the jack and plug in the Fender guitar. He boosted up onto the stool and gave a tug to his ball cap. Deliberately, never looking up from his fingers moving across the frets of his instrument, he played through the 'D', 'G', 'A' progression of the first verse; and then he picked up the tempo a little, fingering the chords for the chorus. Then he began to pray.

It's me again Lord, Prayin' for a friend
We need your help Lord, we need your guiding hand…

He sang about his friend, Wilfred.

He's been strong Lord, and steadfast in his faith
He's been humble and sure to give you praise…

The people in the audience didn't see Wilfred; they saw one of their own friends—some friend who was doing the best he could, but needed God's help. Jacob, the man with the magical guitar, was interceding on their friend's behalf. And then the chorus:

Lord as we face these trying hours
We seek your grace and you're mighty power…

There were only two more short verses—it was a simple song really—all of them could see that. But that's what the Lord wants, they told themselves as they listened again to the chorus, a simple prayer: 'It's me again, Lord, praying for a friend'.

They weren't ready to respond when the singer finished and folded his hands on the body of his guitar. They watched him pull his cap away from his eyes and grin at them. *Go ahead*, the singer told them, without actually saying anything. *Go ahead and applaud!*

And so they did, vigorously, enthusiastically, but maybe somewhat reverently. They applauded; but Jacob didn't seem to hear them. He was stiff, visibly uncomfortable, his face red, distracted, as if he had more to tell them.

Abruptly, he gave a tug at his cap. He was ready again—pay attention!

His fingers began again, this time painting a solitary man, alone in his car. There was a storm brewing; he was late coming home from work.

I pulled in the drive, under stormy skies
I was tired and the hour was late…

As Jacob played and sang, they watched his story unfold, a story about an angel with light coming from his eyes. The light shone into every room of the man's home, uncovering secrets and lost love.

The light shined first on my child as he slept
and I was able to see his dreams
I saw the loves in his heart and the secrets he kept
but none of them included me…

And when the light was turned on the man himself, there was only emptiness and despair.

Then my heart turned cold as I realized
that the light was shining on me
And I knew that the angel with the light in his eyes
was looking where my heart should be...

But wait, his grandfather's bible...he was reading his grandfather's bible.

The light shined last on a dusty shelf
on a book that was old and worn
My grandfather's bible sat all by itself
as I read it my heart grew warm...

This was a Christian Country music audience; they had come to hear Christian music. They were not disappointed!

Their applause was more spontaneous after the second song. Even before Jacob pushed back the bill of his ball cap, they were ready; their applause his reward for a wonderful story.

Tell us another, their applause told the guitar player, *tell us another*!

Jacob pulled a white handkerchief from the back pocket of his jeans, wiping perspiration from his eyes and forehead. His T-shirt was wet but had not yet soaked through to his outer shirt.

With his next song, he prayed again. Rather, he promised to pray.

We will pray for you
sittin' on the back porch in the mornin' sun...

Jacob had a friend, a friend who was going away to be made well. He promised to pray for his friend, he promised that *all* of them would pray.

Was this a concert or church? How did this man, in a simple shirt and worn running shoes...how did he know so much about prayer?

Again they rewarded him with their applause, but again he was impatient. In fact, this time he reached into his shirt pocket and pulled something out while he waited for them to finish applauding. There was an almost inaudible 'beep'.

Then he stuffed—whatever it was—back into his pocket and began again. A little of the redness dissolved from his face after that beep, Jacob was ready for another story. And so were they. Another tug of the cap—they were used to that gesture now, they expected it—and his next story began with a one-word prayer.

Lord, we sure could use a miracle today.

Another story about an angel; this angel was in a mirror.

A voice said: Look into the mirror and tell me what you see. Look beyond your own reflection, where only eyes of faith can see...

And later, in a deep, clear pool of water.

I dreamed I saw a river, where the water was deep and clear
Then a single drop of rain made my reflection disappear...

What a wonderful way to look for answers about life, beyond your own reflection! When he finished his story, they applauded again.

Some of the redness had returned to his face, they could see it when he pushed back his cap. His shirt was sopping wet now, they could see huge drops of sweat running down his cheeks, the back of his arms and hands were glistening in the stage lights.

Jacob hesitated; then began to play again; the tune was up-tempo, something entirely different—yet another story!

But then he stopped, not finishing the instrumental introduction to his song. He looked up, as if searching the audience for someone.

Jacob leaned forward.

"Sorry, that's all I can do tonight..." he told them. He gave a weak smile and reached down to unplug his guitar. Leaning forward again, he paused to look out at them. It seemed an eternity before he said to the now-silent auditorium, "Thanks, everyone. Goodnight."

The applause as Jacob left the stage was deafening.

Thank you the audience was telling him with their ovation. *We know it hurt for you to tell us your stories and to pray with us, but thank you. Thank you, Jacob!*

After three long minutes—maybe they thought Jacob would come back out, do one more song, but it was not to be—Steve, the MC, made an announcement. "Ladies and Gentlemen," he told them, "we'll take a short intermission."

Chapter 22

Clifton Jenson was the first to meet Sonny as he stumbled from the stage. He walked beside him as they made their way to the alcove where Sonny had left the guitar case. He heard several beeps as Sonny fingered buttons on a remote control that he pulled from his shirt pocket.

Right before Clifton's eyes, Sonny's countenance improved. The redness faded from his face and some of the rigidity in his neck and shoulders dissipated. "Are you alright?" he asked.

"Yeah…yeah, I'm okay." Sonny laid John's guitar in one of the big easy chairs and sat in another. He wanted to express his gratitude to the tall cowboy by saying his name, but he couldn't remember it. "Thanks…" he offered his hand.

Clifton shook his hand. The grip was strong; he'd never seen a fellow performer recover so quickly from complete exhaustion. "That had to be the quickest recovery I've ever seen." He pointed at Sonny's controller. "What does that thing do?"

Sonny grinned. "Pain control—works pretty well."

The singer returned the grin. "Yeah, I guess so…

"That was some show you put on out there, Pardner. Me and the boys will really have to be 'on' tonight." He took another look at Sonny's eyes. His gaze was a bit vacant, but the man looked just fine now that his pain gizmo had done its job. "Say, Sonny?"

"Yeah?"

"Y'all are from over near Knoxville. We're scheduled to play at the Knoxville Christian Center on Sunday afternoon. I don't know if Lynne's got anybody lined up yet, Jennie Marie being out for a while.

"I figured I'd ask—it's right there in your neck of the woods—would you mind if I ask Lynne 'bout you opening again for us again Sunday? I'd sure like to have you."

He saw Lynne approaching from his right; Jenny, the good-looking redhead was with her. "I think he's alright now," Clifton told them.

Noticing Lynne's harried expression…"I heard Steve announce the intermission. I'd better get the guys out there—we've got a show of our own to do!"

As Jenson turned to leave, the band's drummer, Sandy was his name, came down the hallway with a white hand towel and a bottle of water.

"Thanks," Sonny told him, twisting the bottle cap. He let out a long breath after gulping a drink. "That helped a lot."

When his elbow bent to use the towel to wipe some of the moisture from the back of his neck, he flinched, feeling a jolt of current from bending his chin forward.

Sonny saw Sandy jump when he twitched. "I'm fine," he hurried to assure him, "just a little twi…twinge. You go ahead; I know you've got a show to do."

****

"How's it going?" Jenny sat down beside her husband.

"Just a little tired," he answered, reaching for her hand. He couldn't stop grinning. "How'd I do?"

She swatted at his hand. "Don't quit your day job…" Then laughed. "You know you did great, you don't need me to tell you."

"Come on, Babe." He smirked, gathering in her hand. "I did real good, didn't I?"

She looked at his eyes. He looked unfocused, the same as other times he'd performed; as soon as the adrenalin wore off, he'd be a basket case. "I guess you did okay." Squeezing his hand, she returned his smile. "Rest a couple more minutes, then we'd better go."

Sonny didn't argue. He took another swig of water and then began undoing the latches of the Fender guitar case.

From what Lynne Lewis could see, Jacob was fine. “Glad he’s alright,” she warily patted Jenny on the shoulder.

Then to Sonny…”Wonderful show, Jacob! Absolutely wonderful! They loved you, the audience absolutely loved you!”

Sonny nodded absently. “Thanks,” he said, gently packing the Stratocaster away.

Lynne had to take care of the rest of the show; it was her job to make certain that the intermission was short and that the show’s star, Clifton Jenson, was ready to perform.

“I’ve got to go. I’ll call you.” She hurried away.

****

Rachel Henson tried to hustle down the outer aisle and follow her friend when she saw Jenny hurry through the wings of the stage area. But without a backstage badge, security would not let her pass through.

As she worked her way back up the aisle, she waved to the rest of the Oak Ridge group, signaling for them to keep their seats. Doug and Jim followed her outside. They walked the length of the now-full parking lot, back to Jim’s Explorer, and piled in to wait for Sonny and Jenny. A strong wind had come up, it was too cold to stand around outside.

****

Another person had witnessed Jenny’s abrupt leaving from her seat. Joel Reed had a Texas Swing Festival in Dripping Springs, near Austin, scheduled for Saturday afternoon. Taking in Sonny’s show meant he’d have to take the redeye flight to Dallas and an early-morning connector to Austin, but Joel wasn’t going to miss Jacob’s performance.

He didn’t want to pass up the chance to more completely understand the man’s music. Joel had downloaded the email attachments that Jenny had passed along to him. He practiced the songs, over and over, memorizing the words and working his way through the guitar chords. His tenor was a whole octave higher than Sonny’s baritone, but he felt comfortable with the songs.

He’d sung along, under his breath, as Sonny performed tonight, trying to master the timing and rhythm. And he hadn’t missed the beep when Sonny adjusted his, whatever it was called—the electronic pain controller. He sensed the struggle the performer was going through and said a silent prayer that he'd find a way to get through it, to get his songs out to the audience.

Joel knew the stage pass routine; he'd played the Gaylord Center several times as a backup singer and guitar player. Knowing he couldn't go to Sonny's aid backstage, he went out the front and walked around to the rear entrance. He was waiting when Jenny and Sonny came out the stage door. "Let me help you with those," he told Sonny, reaching for the guitar cases.

"Oh, Joel, it's you!" Jenny exclaimed, surprised to see him.

Sonny let him take his own battered case but held on to the Fender. "Thanks," he said, "I'll carry this one."

"Hey, I noticed you weren't playing your acoustic. That Stratocaster sounded real good."

"It's John Tyler's," Sonny said, blowing on his free hand as they walked toward the car. "It's cold out here!"

Jenny shrugged into her jacket and held Sonny's guitar case as he put his on.

"John came back…backstage, out of the blue," Sonny told Joel. "He's letting me use it."

"John's quite an encourager, isn't he? We've talked, over the phone, about y'all."

"We didn't know you were coming, Joel!" Jenny said as they started walking toward their car. "If you'd let us know, we'd have tried to work something out with Lynne, maybe got you one of these stage pass dealies." She shook the plastic card, hanging from the lanyard around her neck. "It's nice to see you here."

"Glad to be here, Jenny. I saw you go up through the wings, figured you might need a little help." He studied Sonny's bearing as they walked. He looked worn out.

It was hard for Joel to imagine four songs taking such a toll. *Must be the pain,* he told himself. He lifted his head skyward as they walked. *Lord bless him,* he prayed silently.

****

The waiting friends from Oak Ridge saw Jenny and Sonny leaning into the weather on the way to their car. Sonny had a new-looking guitar case in his hand; a third man, short and stocky, wearing a cowboy hat, was carrying Sonny's own battered guitar case.

Rachel opened the rear passenger door of Jim's car as they approached. "I thought he was hurt or something," she called to Jenny. "You hurried out the side of the stage area down there!"

Jim and Doug got out with her, concern on their faces.

"He's alright now," Jenny answered, reaching to hug her friend. "He just got worn out, all of a sudden."

Pulling at her coat collar against the cold, she turned to introduce Joel. "This is Joel Reed. You remember, Rache, the singer at Tootsies I was telling you about?"

"Nice to meet you, Joel," Rachel said, gesturing toward the others. "This is my husband, Doug, and our friend, Jim Norton."

Jenny hurried to the driver's side of the car to unlock the doors as they exchanged greetings. She reached inside and pressed the button to pop the trunk.

"I thought you were about to collapse," Doug said as he moved to help Sonny with his load.

Sonny gave him a weak smile as they packed the guitars into the trunk. "Nah, I'm alright." Blowing on his hands, he took the time to carefully wrap a blanket around John's guitar case to keep it from getting scratched.

Doug offered to drive them home but Jenny declined. "We're fine," she told him, including Rachel and Jim in her assurance. "The seat folds back; he can rest on the ride home." She nodded toward the entrance to the building. "You should go back in—get out of this wind! Stay and watch the rest of the show."

Turning to Joel, as the others hurried away, Jenny said, "Thanks for being here. It was good of you to come around and help."

"Yeah," Sonny said. "Thanks, Joel."

He paused a moment, wanting to clear his head in all the excitement, then touched Joel's shoulder. "It was a surprise to see you, but your coming…it means more than I can say."

He took a step away from the trunk, closing it. "Listen, I want to talk to you some more about my songs."

Jenny interrupted, "Sonny, we've got to get you out of this cold!"

Struggling to hold her door open against a gust of wind…"Joel, you'll have to forgive us. We'll call you early tomorrow." She ducked behind the wheel.

Joel stepped aside as Sonny got in the passenger seat, and then leaned inside the car. "I've got a show in Austin, Texas, tomorrow," Joel told them. "You can call, but it'll be Monday before I can get back to you.

"Still have my card?"

"Sure do," Sonny assured him. "We'll be in touch."

"Did you say Austin?" Jenny asked. "Shouldn't you be on a flight by now?"

"I'm booked on the redeye." He laughed. "I wouldn't have missed Sonny's show for the world!"

Joel was uncomfortable, squatting to carry on their conversation. "I'll let y'all go," he said, touching Sonny's shoulder. "Keep the faith, Brother!" He closed the door.

****

"Thanks again, for checking on us!" Jenny called, working the automatic window as they drove by their three friends from Oak Ridge—they were nearly back to the auditorium entrance.

"Sure you're alright?" Doug leaned down to meet Jenny's eye. "I can drive if you need me to, Rachel can…"

"Get in out of the cold," Jenny chided, "we'll call you first thing tomorrow!"

****

"I'm sorry we worried them," Sonny told Jenny as they waved, pulling away.

"They're good friends, Hon," his wife answered. "I'm sure it scared Rache when I left my seat and ran backstage."

"I started to do the 'Rainbow' song." Sonny sighed, locating the small pillow they kept in the back seat. He beeped his stimulator twice as he adjusted his seat to the reclining position. "I just ran out of gas."

He reached to touch her neck as she negotiated the turn onto Broadway. "I did what you said, though. I stopped when it got too bad. No sense hurting myself."

Jenny turned to smile at him.

"I did good, though, don't you think?" He grinned.

"You did wonderfully, Sonny!" She reached behind her head to caress the back of his hand. "I was proud of you."

She moved to get out of her jacket, tossing it over into the back seat—the car was warming quickly. "I was proud that you used good judgment, too; stopping when you did."

He unzipped his jacket, too, but kept it on. "I'll get some rest."

There was enough energy for one more enthusiastic remark. "That was fantastic, Babe, hearing all those people applauding…I've never felt like that before!"

"You were wonderful, Hon," she assured him again. "Now get some rest."

****

Sonny woke up abruptly, near Cookeville, not quite half way home. "I need a shower," he told her, as he adjusted his seat and shrugged out of his jacket. "I feel like I pitched twelve innings."

For the remainder of their trip he had the same problem that he'd had after Thursday's recording session, adjusting his controller, up two, down one. Then he'd fidget a while, switching the stereo from the radio to the CD player and back again.

"That was weird, Joel showing up at the back door like that," Jenny said, reaching to turn off the stereo. "Imagine him taking the redeye to Dallas, just so he could hear you sing!"

"Ungh!" was all Sonny answered; he was staring absently out the window.

They stopped at a Wendy's drive-thru on the east end of Crossville and got a burger. Jenny was hungry and finished her meal; her husband was uncharacteristically finicky, leaving more than half his burger. "Fred will eat this," he said, wrapping the remainder.

After that short respite while they ate, Sonny was back at it, more controller adjustments, up then down, down then up. Jenny was ready to jump out the window by the time they reached home.

Chapter 23

He took two Excedrin PM pills and sat down to watch the tube, waiting for the sleep aid to relax him. Sonny was distracted, trying to watch a west coast pro basketball game, still making continual adjustments to the amperage of his neurostimulator.

Rachel called from her cell as their group was driving home from Nashville, wanting to see if there was anything she could do. "I'll give you a call tomorrow," Jenny told her.

Sonny turned off the ball game; he'd not really been paying attention. "I'm gonna take Fred for a walk around the block."

"It's pretty late." Jenny glanced at the clock above the armoire; it read 11:45. She wasn't about to let him go out without her. She hung her robe up in the bedroom and slipped on a sweat suit, to trudge around the block with him. Even Fred wasn't very enthusiastic about a walk at this late hour.

After their walk, Sonny encouraged her to go on to bed. "Maybe I'll read." He picked up the Hiaasen novel she'd been telling him about, but put it back down before Jenny even left the room. "I'll just sit here a while."

She heard him from the bedroom, pacing the floor, then sitting down, his easy chair creaking as he pulled the recline lever. There were beeps, followed by more beeps. Jenny couldn't differentiate between dreamed electronic signals and the real thing. Her husband tried several times to come to bed but kept getting back up; to go to the bathroom or back into the living room and watch Sports Center.

But always, he was making adjustments. Beep followed beep, followed beep!

****

Lynne called early Saturday morning, urging Jenny to go online and read the Entertainment section of Saturday's Tennessean. "Peter Poindexter loved him!" the music producer told her. "But you were there; you know everybody loved Jacob last night!"

"Thanks for calling, Lynne," Jenny said, meaning it. "Sonny and I will look at it together this afternoon, as soon as he's feeling better."

Lynne had more to say, "Peter is hounding me for an interview. We need to set something up over the phone. Also, I chatted with Mr. Randall after last night's show. We need to talk!"

She's only doing her job, Jenny reminded herself, biting her tongue. Aloud she said, "You'll have to give us some time, Lynne. I promise we'll get back to you as soon as we can." And then she hung up.

Sonny had been passed out in the living room when Jenny got up at 7:00 AM. On the kitchen counter, next to the refrigerator, she found a still-open bottle of Bacardi Gold and four 'dead soldier' Heineken bottles. He was in the recliner; the phone ringing didn't wake him. She wasn't about to try to stir him to get him to go to bed. By whatever means, at long last, he was sleeping.

She went into the computer room to read the article Lynne had called about. Peter Poindexter, staff writer for the Entertainment section of the Tennessean, did the story covering Clifton Jenson's Southern Christian music show at the Gaylord Entertainment Center. The article's title was: *Prayer Meeting breaks out at Southern Christian show opener.*

> *'It's me again, Lord!' That's how the tall guy in the baseball cap began his first number. The crowd came to be entertained. Jacob, an unknown from the East Tennessee town of Oak Ridge, gave the audience much more than what they came for. He only sang four songs; that's about all an*

opening act performs, but what songs they were—songs about angels, songs about praying, songs that seemed to tear the red-faced performer's heart out as he sang!

The story went on from there, the remainder mostly about Clifton Jenson's show. His performance had gone well, too.

"Whatcha reading?" Sonny asked, lurching into the room. Before she could answer, he hurried back out, on his way to the bathroom. Sounds of vomiting caused her to rush to the kitchen to fix a large glass of ice water and start the teakettle.

She heard water running; a shower would help, too. What little she'd seen of her husband was alarming: his face was puffy, the whites of his eyes were pink; there was dried spittle on his chin, the sides of his buzz haircut were matted down.

Now, fresh from his shower, at least his face was clean and his hair was bushy again. He gulped his blood pressure pill with the ice water but shook his head when she offered a donut. "What time did you finally get to sleep?" She'd already put the rum bottle back into the fridge and taken the beer bottles outside to the recycle container.

The teakettle whistled. "Ah, nectar of the Gods," Sonny got up to prepare the cups his wife had laid out, cream for his, a spoon of sugar for hers. He looked at the countertop. "I see you cleared away the evidence."

He shook his head, working at the cobwebs, as he brought the cups to the table. "Back to old habits…"

Jenny touched the back of his hand with her fingertips. "Whatever it takes, Hon."

After a couple minutes of quiet time, enjoying the coffee, he started fidgeting. "I've got to turn on my…" He got up and went to the living room. Jenny heard him walking around, his bare feet slapping lightly on the hardwood.

Several beeps and three minutes later he reappeared, holding the controller out in front of him. "This thing about shocked me on my butt! I must have had it turned…"

Instead of finishing his sentence, he laid the device on the table and picked up his coffee cup. Pushing buttons on the microwave, he reheated his coffee then sat down again. "What time is it?"

Jenny looked at the clock on the stovetop. "A little after nine. Do you want some juice?" He had finished the ice water when he first sat down; he shook his head at the OJ offer. "Breakfast? Oatmeal maybe?" He shook his head again. "Lynne called this morning, telling me about a newspaper story on the Internet. I was reading through it when you woke up. It was in the Enter…"

Her husband suddenly pushed away from the table and dropped his head and hands to his lap. "Ouch!" He sat back up abruptly, jolted by the dropping of his chin.

He stood and picked up the controller, clumsily pulling his arm back in a throwing motion.

"Sonny!" Jenny exclaimed, jumping up to catch his wrist.

He relaxed his arm, slumping back into the chair. He put his chin in his palm, elbow on the table, the posture that allowed for maximum amperage. "I gotta get some sleep," he mumbled.

Jenny left the room and came back with the Excedrin PM bottle. "It's been long enough since you took the other ones." She set the pills on the table and went to the sink to pour a half-glass of water.

He shook his head. "They didn't work last night."

"That was last night. You were pretty wired last night, what with being a big music star and all." She patted his arm, catching his cloudy gaze. "Take a couple of those." She gestured at the pills. "Then I'll tuck you in."

After swallowing the pills…" I've still got a little coffee left. Oh, I need to call Jim. The guys have got a Region game this afternoon. Powell, I think."

Jenny knew the Baseball Wildcats schedule as well as her husband. "That's Monday, Sonny."

He looked at her, not completely focusing. "What's today?"

"Saturday."

"Oh." He picked up his controller and headed for the bedroom.

****

When he came down to her sewing room at a little after 1:30 in the afternoon, some of the pinkeye was gone. Jenny had heard water running and noticed that Sonny had shaved. There were two dabs of Kleenex hanging from his chin, blotting minor cuts. "You going with us?" he asked.

"With who?"

"Me and Jim, I'll get him to drive."

"Where are we going?"

Sonny huffed impatiently. "The Powell game, I told you before I laid down. Come on if you're going, it's almost an hour ride and I want to watch them warm up." He pulled the controller from his shirt pocket, beeping twice, glancing at his shoulders as always, tracing the current with his eyes. Her husband was still in his Jockey's; he had on the long-sleeved shirt he'd worn to the Gaylord performance, and no shoes or socks.

Jenny got up from her sewing machine, flicking off the console light. "Why don't we just go for a walk instead? Fred has been missing you today. Come upstairs with me, I need to put on my tennies."

She got her husband into some jeans and a pullover sweatshirt before their walk. The Kleenex swabs had dried the cuts; he splashed some cold water on his face before they left. He didn't mention the Powell game.

"I have to go to the grocery store. What do you want for supper?" Jenny tried to make conversation as they walked. Sonny was shuffling along, letting Fred pull at the leash.

All of a sudden, Fred yelped. "Sonny!" Jenny yelled. "Don't yank like that! You'll jerk his neck off. Give me the leash!"

Sonny handed her the leash without comment, and turned in the other direction. "I'm tired," he murmured, "I'm going home and go back to bed."

Jenny and Fred turned with him to walk back the way they'd come.

****

"Do we have Joel's number somewhere?" Sonny called from the bedroom at a little after 5:00 PM.

Jenny was in the kitchen, on the phone with Lynne, for the third time today. Not very patiently she had told the young woman that yes, she'd read the Tennessean article, but no, Sonny still wasn't available for a conference call.

"All this will just have to wait until Monday, Lynne," she finally said. Hearing Sonny, she brought the call to a close. "Please don't call any more this weekend."

As she hung up, her husband called again, louder this time. "What are you yelling about?" she asked, walking into the bedroom. He was sitting on the edge of the bed, beeping his controller, holding his back perfectly straight.

He pointed to his mouth and shuffled to the bathroom to put his teeth in. Coming back to get dressed, he asked again, "Don't we have Joel's number somewhere? He said we could call him, remember? Where did you put his business…"

"I've got his card in my purse, Hon." Jenny knew, as her husband should have, that Joel would be in Texas over the weekend. He had asked that they wait until Monday to try to reach him.

She tried to change the subject. "I got some hamburger and gravy mix at the store while you were asleep. Do you want to eat early? You haven't eaten anything today."

Sonny paid no attention to her question. He pulled his jeans from the bedpost, putting them on, reaching for his sweatshirt. "I didn't really expect him to come to our…" he said from under the sweatshirt, pulling it on.

Looking at her again…"We need his help to get my, er, I mean, *your* songs written."

Jenny overlooked the mistake, he meant 'published'. "I'll go fix supper. There's surely some college game on. Come and get some milk after you get through in the bathroom."

When he came into the kitchen, Sonny started fishing around in his wife's purse.

"Just a minute." She gently took it from his hands, finding Joel's business card.

Sonny had his cell phone with him. He turned it on and dialed the number on the card. After a moment he left his name and number on Joel's answering machine, shaking his head as he got up to pour a glass of milk. "I thought sure he'd be around."

He shrugged. "What are you making?"

"Hamburger gravy."

"It's kinda early for supper. Are you hungry already?" He read the stove's clock. "It's only quarter after five." He paused, drinking some milk. "I could eat, though.

"Hey, want to see if Doug and them want to go out for dinner later?"

Jenny pulled away from the stove and gave him a hug. "Maybe tomorrow," she said. "Why don't you go turn on a game until I get supper ready?"

****

Sonny took another dosage of sleeping aids—thank goodness the label said they weren't habit forming—and went back to bed around 8:30 that Saturday evening. The fever and night sweats were back.

He tried to think back…how long since his last relapse? *Today is Saturday. The last time it was three days—last Friday, and over the weekend.* He'd never had two periods of exhaustion occur so close together. *This can't be good.*

With only intermittent trips to the bathroom and a couple of Heinekens after lunch, he slept most of the day Sunday. Jenny didn't attempt to say much to him during periods when he was awake, wanting to avoid the disappointment of more nonsensical, disjointed dialogue.

She managed to get away for coffee with Rachel on Sunday, after the Henson's got home from church. Talking things through, giving voice to her concerns about Sonny's condition, helped a little. "It's been less than a week since his last bad spell, Rache. It's never happened twice in a month, no less in the same week. This messing with his neurostimulator is really bad for him!"

"Seems like making music is important to him, though, Jen…He seems to have more—what? Purpose? Joy of living?"

"Yes, I know. That's what so bad. It's like the music has given him a new reason to be alive. After his being down for so long, I'm really glad. But it worries me. It worries me a lot!"

"Do you think it's doing permanent damage?"

"Based on the times before, I don't *think* it will be permanent. He always seems to bounce back after his body shuts down to recover," she told her friend. "But let me ask you something else. Do you think he's stammering a lot—forgetting words, stuff like that?"

"I can't tell. You're around him so much more than anyone else."

"Oh, remember that exam I told you about, that the psychiatrist did for Intercom Insurance? I requested they send a copy to Dr. Gupta. I really want to see what a professional thinks of all his forgetting and stuff."

"That should help, Jen. Maybe it will give you both a different perspective."

Chapter 24

Jenny called and asked for a substitute for her Monday morning volunteer assignment at the hospital. The phone woke Sonny at around 9:00 that morning; she had been up since 6:30, filling Fred's water and food bowls, dusting, mopping the kitchen floor—anything to occupy her time. Finally she went downstairs to wrap a package to send to Hailey. Hailey was the 4-year-old daughter of one of her sister Lisa's sons, Blake, an air traffic controller in Denver. Hailey loved the hand-sewn dresses her great-aunt sewed for her.

It was probably Lynne on the phone; Jenny let the answering machine pick up. She heard her husband stirring and hurried upstairs. She'd been impatient to see him this morning, hoping the relapse was over.

"Please, God…" she heard herself say as she climbed the stairs. *Where did that come from?* She remembered Joel's urging Sonny to 'keep the faith'. *Must be rubbing off on me,* she thought.

He looked better, much better. The puffiness was gone, his eyes were clear. His movements were no longer sluggish. Another recovery!

Jenny drank some of her Pepsi while Sonny dunked his donut. "I stayed home today, in case you were still tired."

He touched the controller in his pocket. "I'm down to around two-point-five or so today, about back to normal." He shook his head. "This was strange, though, being down again so soon…Seems like it's been less than a week since the last re…relapse; that's not good."

He expected his wife to comment. She was looking out the window, avoiding his gaze. She felt almost guilty—studying her husband's responses. *Is he stammering? Is he making sense?*

"Well, anyway, I'm back up and at 'em. You want to go along to the Powell game this afternoon?"

"Sure, I guess. Maybe Karen will go, if Jim is going."

Sonny took a final sip of orange Juice. "I'll have to call and leave a mess…message for Jim at the office. We've been trying to get together since he came over and loaded that soft…soft…that *stuff* on the computer.

"I wish we'd have been able to go out somewhere Friday night, after…What's that guy's name?"

He's passing with flying colors! "You mean Clifton?"

"Yeah, that Jenson's a nice guy." Another thought came to mind; he glanced up at the calendar. "You know what?"

Jenny let her spine slip down against the back of her wooden kitchen chair, relaxing for the first time in what seemed like an eternity. "What, Hon?" she smiled.

"Jenson, he said he liked my…act? Anyway, he said I should ask Lynne about opening for him again, someplace in Knoxville."

Jenny didn't want to break up his good mood but her face let her down, she frowned. *Don't start this again...*

Sonny didn't notice her expression. "I think he said it was Sunday afternoon." He shook his head, gesturing at the calendar. "Yesterday.

"Oh well, we miss…missed that one. Has that woman called you this weekend, about the show and all?"

Jenny picked up his glass and cup along with her Pepsi glass, carrying them to the sink. As expected, she saw a '1' on the message counter of the answering machine. "Lynne called and nagged me most of the day Saturday. I told her she'd have to wait until you were feeling better. I think that was her, leaving a message, when I came upstairs while ago. I heard you stirring around, so I let the machine pick up." She didn't reach for the phone.

"Let me call and leave a message for Jim at school about the game." He looked out the window. "Looks like it's a pretty day, what's the weath…weatherman say?"

Jenny was rinsing the glasses, putting them in the dishwasher. "I don't know."

After Sonny finished his call, she asked if he wanted to catch up on their computer messages. "We got three emails over the weekend. Come on, you'll like them.

"Oh," she said as they walked through the living room, carrying the phone in case Lynne called again. "I marked a 'favorite' for a newspaper article about your show. It was in Saturday's Entertainment section of the Tennessean, the Nashville paper."

"Let's look at the newspaper thing first." Sonny couldn't help but smirk, looking over her shoulder as she double-clicked Internet Explorer. He read the newspaper story aloud until the critique switched emphasis to Clifton's part of the show. "That's nice. The part about 'giving more than they came for'."

Jenny selected 'Print' from the menu. "I need to print this, send it to Mom and Lisa."

Lisa, Jenny's sister, was married to a Delta Airlines pilot and lived in Atlanta. Jenny's mother had moved into a mother-in-law apartment added on to the rear of Lisa's home in the early '90s.

Without waiting while the paper worked its way through, Jenny toggled to the email software. The messages were lined up, based upon when they were received.

From: lynne@SouthernChristian.com
Date: Saturday, April 2, 2005, 9:07 AM
To: Sonnyandjen@bellsouth.net
Subject: Urgent message!

Dear Jenny and Sonny,

Wonderful job last night, Jacob!

I've been trying to reach you! We need to talk, ASAP!

Peter Poindexter, of the Tennessean, wants to set up a three-way over the phone!

Thanks!

Lynne

PS Mr. Randall called me this morning! Very unusual, on a Saturday! He wants to include one of Jacob's songs on our next compilation disk!

"Like I told you," Jenny commented, "she's been bugging me. We'll check the answering machine in a few minutes."

"Every sentence ends with an ex…exclamation point. That's 'Lee-anne', nothing if not enthusiastic, even in her email. What's next?" Sonny wanted to know.

From: Toniclarkston@Countryconnections.com
Date: Saturday, April 2, 2005, 11:15 AM
To: Sonnyandjen@bellsouth.net
Cc: Joel@joelReed.com,
JohnTyler@tootsies.net,
Subject: You're in the news!

Dear Jenny and Sonny,

In case you've not seen this yet, here's a link to the local newspaper. Seems Pete Poindexter likes your style.

TennesseanEntertainmentSection.com/april22005…

Thanks for copying me on your song submittals to RMG. John T. and Joel have been keeping me informed about your progress, too. Good work! Don't know if John mentioned it, we're doing a lot of the 'house band' work at Tootsies. Saves driving all over town to find work.

I'm still working on CeeCee. I'm going to send her this link. I've already sent her an attachment of one of the angel songs you sent to Lynne. Hope you won't mind.

Looking forward to hearing more good things about Jacob (Sonny, really, of course!).

I'll be in touch,
Toni (you can call me Rhonda if you'd rather—lol!)

"Rhonda Bixwell," Jenny said. "One of the truly great performer names of all times."

"Pretty exciting about CeeCee, huh? Jim was saying she and—I think her husband's name is BeeBee—they're big in Gos…Gospel music. That would be something, to perform with them. We could really sell our songs if we…"

Jenny turned back to the screen to hide the emotions on her face. *I wish you'd never perform again!* was what she wanted to say. Instead, she said aloud, "You never know what might happen, I guess."

****

Before Jenny could bring up the next email message, the phone rang, there on the computer desk. "Probably Lynne again," she said. "Hello?"

She held the phone away from her ear. With Lynne's piercing voice, Sonny could easily overhear. "Hi Jenny, it's Lynne. I waited 'til this mornin', like you asked. We have a whole lot to talk about."

"Sonny's right here," she replied. "Go ahead."

They heard her inhale deeply, working into it. "Goodness, y'all, where do I start? I'm sure y'all have read Peter Poindexter's article in the Tennessean, haven't you?" They both replied affirmatively.

"Well, the whole town is talking about you, Jacob. We need to strike while the iron is hot, as they say."

She had talked with Peter Saturday evening, telling him that Jacob wouldn't be available until at least Monday morning. 'It'll be old news by then,' the Entertainment section writer had told her—no sense bringing that up now…

Lynne pressed on. "When Jenny said you'd be unavailable until today, I went ahead and booked Melanie Rayborn as Clifton's opening act last night. It's too bad you missed that one, Jacob, the show was right there close to home at the Knoxville Christian Center."

Lynne paused, waiting for a reply, but got none.

"Oh well, water under the bridge," she said, stretching 'bridge' into two syllables to make it fit her melodic cadence. "Clifton's next appearance is Friday evenin' at the Billy Graham Center, over in Asheville. I looked it up. That's less than a hundred miles from y'all." She cruised along, giving her spiel, "Of course, we'll need to have some CDs available this time! We'd have sold a *thousand* last Friday, after your show!

"Now if we hurry, we can put together a compilation disk with a couple of other new talents I'm working with and have them available by Friday. We'd need to get you in to our studios this afternoon. We usually charge nine hundred per song, but we can come up with a package discount if we do all five songs. And then, we need to put together a media press kit, to get the compilation disk out on the radio…"

"Lynne?" Jenny interrupted.

"Yes?" Sugar in her voice…

Jenny shook her head and grimaced at Sonny. "Lynne, do you ever pay any attention to anything Sonny and I say to you?"

Sonny gave her an exaggerated bob of his head, his eyes wide, urging her on.

She didn't wait for Lynne to reply. "One, we've not given you the go-ahead about any more performances—with Clifton or anyone else, for that matter.

"Two, as I've explained, Sonny is not in the financial position to make any CDs. He can't take any money. Period. Ever. Are we getting through this time, Lynne?"

Her answer was smug. "There are ways to get around your financial concerns."

"Third," Jenny went on, ignoring the reply, "we're certainly not going to pay RMG any money, for a compilation disk or anything else.

"And lastly, as we've told you many times, Custom Sound is our recording studio."

Sonny gave Jenny a thumb's up, whispering, "That's telling her."

It was several long moments before Lynne replied. Her tone changed entirely, now sounding like the thin, all-business blonde they'd met at RMG's offices. "Ms. Jacobs, I have several items on my desk that need my attention. I wonder if we could make an appointment, set a time for me to call you back, later this afternoon?"

Jenny looked the question of what time at Sonny. "We'll have to leave by two o'clock for the ballgame," he told her.

Jenny said into the phone, "Let's make it about twelve-thirty our time. How would that be?"

"I'll call you then," was the terse reply.

****

Lynne rocked back in her office chair. She was used to volatile artists; it was part of the business. She was proud of her ability to turn temperamental performers around. They always had two simple objectives, fame and fortune. RMG's business plan was to get the client to spend, up front, and make sure that after they hit the big time, RMG was in position to expand their own profits.

Jenny Jacobs wasn't giving an inch. She wouldn't pay for promotional services, she wouldn't pay for tracking, and she already had another recording studio. Nor would she let her husband take any payment for performing! She was passing up an opportunity to make money, lots of money, with her attitude. How could whatever paltry sum he was making on disability compare to the promise of a lucrative recording contract?

And what was the deal with Jacob not being available over the weekend? His 'that's all I can do tonight' as he left the stage Friday was great theater! Leave 'em wanting more...It was all part of his 'Aw shucks' act. He'd looked a little rough at the end of that last number, but in just the few moments it had taken for them to make it backstage he was completely relaxed, sipping his bottled water.

'What's the bottom line?' was one of Leroy Randall's favorite questions. *Okay, what does Jenny want, what's her bottom line?* Lynne turned to her computer keyboard and brought up the very first email she had received from Jenny Jacobs.

Dear Lynne,

Attached is a recording of "Angel With The Light In His Eyes." This was one of the songs performed by Jacob at Tootsies, on Sunday, March 20th. I believe you have been contacted by Joel Reed and John Tyler about the GREAT response the song received.

As the copyrighted author of the song, I am requesting that you evaluate the recording and contact me concerning the possibility of publication.

Jenny Jacobs

There, in the last sentence, was her answer. Lynne didn't believe for a moment that Jenny wrote those songs. Yet, she had the copyright. Jenny wanted to get those songs published—she wanted to be recognized as the songwriter. *Fame and fortune,* Lynne told herself, *the game never changes.* It was time to try a new tactic with Jenny Jacobs.

****

"She just doesn't get it, does she?" Sonny asked his wife after their conversation with Lynne.

Jenny shook her head. "It's laughable! She assumed we were just sitting by the phone, waiting for her call to tell us where to play next. And we're supposed to drive back to Nashville and make that Compilation Disk, for the mere sum of…how much did she say?"

Sonny blinked. "I don't know. I know RMG's out to get as much of our money as they can."

He touched her shoulder; she was still in the chair at the computer terminal. "You did good! What do you think she wants to tal…talk about? When she calls back?"

"When she first got on the phone I thought she wanted to set up some sort of conference call with that newspaper columnist. She said he called her, but she didn't mention the conference call this time." Jenny raised her palms in a 'who-knows' gesture, turning back to the email software on her screen. "You can bet when she calls back she'll be trying to use that interview or some other way to get you to perform again."

She didn't let him see her face as she asked, "Do you want to?"

Sonny let go of her shoulder, lying back on a pillow. He beeped once, to alleviate some of his anxiety. He didn't hurry his answer.

He knew his wife was pretending to be busy, bringing up the next email, to hide her expression from him. "Jenny, look at me, please."

She turned; her eyes were wet. She came and sat beside him on the day bed, folding into his arms.

"I know," he whispered, holding her.

After a long, quiet moment together…"I know," he said again.

She straightened her shoulders and sat back on the middle pillow, looking directly into his eyes. "Do you want to keep performing, Sonny?"

"It was bad this time, Jen. I had plenty of time to think while I was…sick." He looked away.

There was only one answer to her question. If he continued to abuse his device, it would do irreparable damage. The neurostimulator was working wonderfully, giving him real relief from his pain—that would have to be enough. The music, performing…it was wonderful. But, no, he couldn't keep abusing his health! *No more!*

"Jenny, I don't think I should try to do any more…" He looked at her, needing a word.

She didn't answer his prompting. Whatever he said had to come from within himself.

Sonny shook his head. "I can't do any more…shows.

"Like I did at Tootsies and the other night…no more, I just can't do it. That many songs, that much pressure…The days after are just too awful. I know it upset you to see me so…sick. And I'm sorry."

She looked at her folded hands, allowing him to finish without input from her.

"For both our sakes, Jen, I won't do any more shows." He pulled her chin up into his hands. "You still remember the joke about peeking in the choir loft?"

She nodded.

"But if someone asked me to sing just one song? I might do it…" He grinned, letting go of her chin. "Just to promote your music, of course."

Jenny didn't laugh but her eyes said that his answer was acceptable—that was good enough for Sonny.

"Let's look at that last email." He got up to sit in the computer chair.

From: JohnTyler@tootsies.net
Date: Sunday, April 3, 2005, 1:17 PM
To: Sonnyandjen@bellsouth.net
Subject: No subject

Dear Sonny and Jenny,
Attaboy Sonny!
TennesseanEntertainmentSection.com/april22005…
John T.

"That was nice, don't you think?" Jenny asked. "For John to encourage you, send you the newspaper article?"

"Sure was," Sonny agreed, getting up from the terminal. "Let me get dressed and take Fred for a short one before Lynne calls back," Sonny said. He caught her look. "Only two miles…" He patted his not-quite-washboard belly. "I'm putting on weight. All this lay…laying around, being sick. I need to get out and move around some, get some vitamin D."

She nodded.

"It'll be good to get away this afternoon," he told her. "Go see the guys play a little ball. Maybe we can start get…getting our lives back to normal."

Jenny laughed now. "What's normal?"

****

Back in the kitchen, after Sonny and Fred left for their walk, Jenny absently listened to Lynne's old message on the answering machine and erased it. The clock on the stove read 10:15; there was time to make her famous 'scratch' soup. They'd have an early lunch, be ready for Lynne's next call, and then go to the ballgame.

It would be good to get 'back to normal'. She was running out of patience with this whole music business. Driving to Nashville what seemed like every other day, spending money for recordings and electronic devices they'd never dreamed of, RMG constantly pressing for money and more performances.

To be fair, they'd met some wonderful people along the way. Joel was caring, as well as talented, and tried to be helpful. Toni was doing her best to get something going from her end, however far-fetched. John had lent Sonny his prize guitar. And good-ol'-boy Jerry would probably be a lifelong friend of Sonny's, even if they never sold a recording.

In the end, though, it was about Sonny. He finally understood—she hoped—that his music was dangerous! Upping the amperage, especially for such long periods, under such intense stress, was too much for his body to bear. But, no more…*no more. No more!*

"I'm holding you to it this time, Sonny," she said aloud, there by herself, peeling potatoes for her soup. But then she shook her head and laughed. *Who am I kidding? It's his music. And it is wonderful music!*

Chapter 25

Sonny was worn out from his short walk. "I'll take a shower and get an hour or so of rest."

By noon, he was back up from his nap. They had just finished lunch when the phone rang.

"To be quite candid, Jenny..." Lynne Lewis began their conversation at exactly 12:30. "I've been reviewing my notes from our previous communications." She was the never-too-thin-never-too-rich Lynne this time, no silly sing-song rhythm, no extra-syllable words.

"What finally has become clear to me is that your main goal is to have your songs *published*." She was careful to tread lightly on the 'your' in her sentence, heavy on 'published'.

Sonny's face brightened, listening in again at the kitchen table. 'Published'; maybe she was finally getting it.

"We're with you so far," Jenny answered.

"Ultimately, that's what we do here at RMG. We represent a number of artists who, for the most part, compose and perform their own music. But we also represent a *few* songwriters, like yourself, Jenny, who do not perform." She paused, making her case. "I emphasize the 'few'. These are songwriters with the prior backing of established performers, through their own, personal contacts. A songwriter doesn't simply hang out a sign, 'open for business'."

"Tell us something we don't know." Sonny laughed into the receiver.

"That's where you come in, Jacob," Lynne said, glad he was going along. "We need *exposure*. We need to get Jenny's songs out there, noticed by people like Peter Poindexter in the Tennessean."

Sonny watched his wife's expression change abruptly. She'd heard something; he'd missed it, whatever it was. Jenny's face was bright pink, on its way to purple. *Look out, Lynne!*

Lynne kept talking, the tempo of her voice accelerating. "Jenny, we need to get your songs radio play time. We need to get you guest spots on local talk shows, radio and TV. We need word-of-mouth advertising, the kind that comes from *live* performances of *your* songs, Jenny!"

Jenny took a deep breath. "Let me see if I understand you?"

*Here it comes…*Sonny watched and listened.

"As I mentioned earlier…" Lynne went on from her end, confident now, ignoring Jenny's attempt to interrupt. "We need to get going on that compilation disk, put together your media press kit; set your songs up for tracking…"

Jenny's interruption was stronger this time. "Hold it!" she yelled into the phone.

"Just listen to what you're saying, would you? Do you think I'm some stupid, star-struck kid?" She stopped, taking a calming breath, wanting to be sure she was understood.

Her voice was flat now, her words pinched into tiny, sharp phrases. "You think this is about *me*? Are you advising me to endanger my husband's health to pursue my own agenda? You dangle promises in front of me like I'm a child, radio time, talk shows.

"What are you implying, Lynne? That I'm some pathetic self-absorbed redhead, willing to sabotage my husband's health to get my name on a record label?"

Jenny was on her feet now, strangling the phone, stomping her foot, yelling again. "How *idiotic* do you think I am?"

"Jenny…er, Ms. Jacobs…" Lynne burbled, "I never meant…"

Before Lynne could continue, Sonny took the receiver from Jenny's hand. "You'd best forget making any further contact with us," he told the music producer. Then he pushed the 'End' button.

His wife rushed out the kitchen door, visibly shaking. "I can't *stand* to be treated like that!" she was saying, "…how could she be so patronizing? So condescending!"

Sonny watched as she paced out to the sidewalk and back. When she came back toward him, he stepped out and grabbed her in a bear hug. "I'm proud of you, Babe, for sti…sticking up for yourself. For both of us!"

Chapter 26

The Wildcats were ahead by 7 runs after the top of the third inning. Karen wasn't all that excited about wasting paid-babysitter time watching a blowout. "We'll catch you guys on the flip-flop," Karen said as she and Jenny made their way down the bleachers.

"Where you headed?" Jim wanted to know.

"Shopping," the two women said together. They laughed.

"We'll stop at The Colonel and get something for supper," Jenny added. "We'll eat around, what? Eight or so?"

The men nodded and waved, distracted. "Did you score that an error or a hit?" Jim asked Sonny, looking over his shoulder at the scorebook.

****

Ten-run rule high school baseball games are short; the guys were back at the house on Upsal by 7:30 PM. "See what's on ESPN," Sonny told Jim, pointing to the remote on the coffee table. "I'll get us a beer."

"Hawks and New Orleans," Jim called from the living room. "They're in the first half. I think Tennessee baseball is finishing their series at Kentucky; they were rained out Sunday. It might be on CSS or FSN."

As Sonny pulled icy mugs out of the freezer, he noticed the message light on the phone. He pressed the button as he poured.

"Mr. and Mrs. Jacobs, you don't know me…" the message began.

It was a woman's voice. *"My name is Miranda Hendricks. I'm calling, let's see, it's about four, that would be five your time, Monday afternoon. I'm an associate producer with Great American Country television—GAC? I think we're Channel 54 over in your part of the state. Anyway, could you give me a call? I'll be available most of the evening. My cell number is: area code 615, 436-0987. That's Miranda Hendricks. Bye."*

Sonny blinked a couple of times, careful not to spill foam over the edge of the mug. "Did you hear that?" he called to his friend in the other room.

"What?"

Sonny walked in with the beers. "Strange message on the answering machine." He gestured at the TV screen. "I thought we were watching the SEC game?"

Jim had cruised back to ESPN. "Nah, CSS is in love with Miami, they were showing a rerun of a game with Clemson from Saturday. I'm back to the Hawks."

Sonny was just standing there, holding the mugs in suspended animation. "You going to give me one of those?" Jim asked from the couch where he was sitting.

"What? Oh, yeah, sorry. Did you hear that message?"

Jim didn't answer; he was busy trying to pick up the score of the game.

"The answering machine message..." Sonny handed his friend a mug but remained standing, still distracted. "A TV...I forget what she said she was, but it's some TV person calling."

Jim couldn't understand him over the noise of the game. "Sorry, I was trying to...Never mind." He pressed 'Mute' and looked up. "What are you saying?"

"Come and listen to this message with me." Sonny walked from the room without looking to see if Jim was following. He pressed the message button again and let it play.

"Associate producer, huh? TV, wow!"

Sonny shook his head. "Doesn't matter...I told Jenny I wouldn't sing any more."

Jim pursed his lips, serious. "You were pretty sick this weekend, huh? I called a couple times; she said you were down for the count."

Sonny sat down at the kitchen table, swallowing some of his Heineken. "We're worried about what it does when I up the juice on my neuro…" He touched his shirt pocket. "This thing."

Jim nodded.

"I get sick, like from ex…exhaustion. You know that," he continued. "But Jenny is worried about the way I talk sometimes—the forgetting…"

Jim sat down with him. "You seem alright to me now."

He paused, but Sonny didn't have anything more to add. "So, this TV thing, you're not interested?"

Sonny laughed. "Are you kidding? Of course I'm interested! I don't even know what it is, but I'm interested!" The pitch of his voice rose. "Who…who wouldn't want to sing on TV? They'd probably only want, like…one or two songs.

"Maybe I could convince Jen."

Jim raised his beer mug. "To 'Jacob', the TV star!"

"Wait!" Sonny scratched his neck, feeling a twinge. He beeped once and waited for it to take effect. "Ahh…"

Jim had seen it before, his friend's reaction to the pain device, but it was still an amazing phenomenon. It was like watching a man receive an injection; Sonny's eyes tracing the current flow out to his shoulders. "That thing really works!"

"Sure does." Sonny took a drink. His expression darkened again. "Oh, I bet I know what this is…You remember that Lynne woman, at the Gay…at the place in Nashville?"

"The one that didn't put your name on the marquee?"

"Yeah. Jenny looked up this…what's the TV network's name?"

"GAC, Great American Country. I've watched them before. They're like CMT, they play Country videos."

Sonny nodded. "Jenny looked them up. I think she said the same…same guy owned all that stuff. Jenny and Lynne had this big fight on the phone."

Jim raised his eyebrows.

"She thought she was play…playing her for a dumb redhead! She really blew up!" Sonny laughed.

"I bet Lynne called this other lady—another way to get me to sing again."

He got up and started toward the living room. "Who's winning the game?"

"Hawks were up by six, a minute ago," Jim answered, releasing the 'Mute' function, so they could hear the announcers.

****

"Hey," Jim said to Karen as the women came in with sacks of KFC. "Sonny might get to sing on TV!"

"Really?"

"What are you talking about?" Jenny wanted to know, leading everyone into the kitchen. She noticed the message light on the machine as she laid her load on the counter. "Who's this from?" she asked Sonny.

"Some TV station."

Their own TV, in the living room, was still blaring out basketball action, Sonny turned as he answered. "Let me go shut that off."

"Aren't you going to listen to the message?" Jim urged.

Jenny pushed the 'Play' button.

The three of them listened, gathered around the answering machine speaker. Sonny came back into the room as the woman's voice left her cell number.

"It's pretty late." Jenny glanced at the stovetop clock. "We'll call her in the morning."

She and Karen set about opening plastic tops on the KFC to-go containers. "Hon, want to get the drinks?"

****

"I was telling Jim," Sonny said, plopping a helping of mashed potatoes on his plate, "I think Lynne at RMG set up that call. Didn't we find that GAC ca…cable network was tied some kind of way to that Randall guy?"

The last thing Jenny wanted to talk about was Sonny performing again, especially in front of their friends. She waved her hand in dismissal. "We'll talk about it tomorrow."

She changed the subject. “We bought a CD burner, Jim. I installed it all by myself. All I did was put the software CD in and follow the directions.”

Jim raised his eyebrows again, a favorite gesture. “Cool.”

“She…burned?” Sonny looked for his wife’s nod; ‘burned’ was the right term. “She burned a duplicate of our copyright CD so we can listen to it in the car. She’s getting good at this tech…techy stuff.”

Karen wasn’t into techy stuff. “It was good to have you come to women’s group last Wednesday, Jenny.” She nodded toward Sonny. “Jim said you were under the weather Sunday.

“Oh, that reminds me, did y’all hear about Stan? We put him on our prayer list Sunday.”

“Stan Hamilton, the chemistry teacher?” Sonny asked.

Karen nodded.

“They think it might be pancreatic cancer.” Jim shook his head gravely. “That’s about the worst kind you can get.”

“When did they find out?”

“They thought it was maybe appendicitis or something. They’re not going to operate until they shrink it some, Mary told me,” Karen said. “He’s already started chemo.”

“I thought you guys were pretty close.” Jim gestured with his fork at Sonny. “Didn’t you play together in the city golf tournament a couple years ago?”

“Yeah, we placed second—he carried me. Stan was my assistant in baseball, back when I was first star…starting out. He played second base for Van…Vandy, knows everything there is to know about the double play pivot.”

He paused, remembering. “When Todd, his oldest, got to junior high, Stan decided to get out of coaching. He wanted to let him make it on his own.

“I haven’t even talked to Stan since…well, since I stopped teach…teaching.”

“Is he at home or in the hospital?” Jenny asked.

“He’s at home.” Karen answered.

“I’ll give Mary a call later,” Sonny said, pushing a half-eaten chicken breast around on his plate, no longer hungry, "maybe I can go by and see him."

"Well, anyway..." Karen tried to break the somber mood. "It was good having you both back in church."

"It's because of you guys," Jenny said, as her husband nodded in agreement. "You, Doug and Rache, some others...We've been kinda isolated, but it seems like everyone has been so good about encouraging us. About Sonny's music, about his getting better with his implant."

She smiled at Karen. "It's good to be back."

"Lord willing..." Sonny laughed. "We'll try to come as much as my health will allow."

Chapter 27

Tuesday morning, before they had a chance to discuss the message from Miranda Hendricks, they got a call from Sherry, Dr. Gupta's receptionist. Their office had received a document from Intercom Insurance. "Something from a Dr. Greene," Sherry told Jenny, "there's a form letter from you, requesting it be sent to us."

"How soon can we come and look at it?"

"Dr. Gupta will have to review it with you, of course." There was a delay while she looked at the appointment book. "We've got a cancellation at nine this morning, otherwise it will be Thursday."

Jenny looked at the clock. 8:15. "We'll be there at nine."

Her husband was in the shower; he'd have to hurry with his coffee this morning.

****

"There are six pages," the roly-poly family practice physician said. His dark complexion suggested an East Indian heritage, but there was no stilted English accent; Dr. Gupta spoke like a native East Tennessean.

He handed the pages to Sonny, seated on the edge of the examining table. "Like most such exams, it's divided into sections: General Information, History, Current Symptomatology…"

"Current what?" Sonny asked, paging through the document, looking for the heading. "Oh, here it is…" He read the first sentence of the section aloud, "'Client has had no prior treatment for mental health symptoms; however, he presented as a severely depressed individual.'

"That's enough for me." Sonny dropped his eyes and thrust the papers toward his wife.

Jenny got up from her chair, in the corner of the examination room, to take the papers from her husband. She forced a smile. "You were having a bad day that day, don't you remember? That was the Monday after we got back from Tootsies; you were dead on your feet."

She handed the document back to the doctor and moved to stand with her hand on Sonny's shoulder. "Why don't we just let Dr. Gupta tell us what it says, in layman's terms?"

Doctor Gupta shuffled the papers to the next-to-last page. "The Medical Assessment section is what's important." He waited until his patient straightened and looked at him. "If you were having one of your 'bad' days, as Jenny says, the results are going to be stilted that way. You're not nearly as alert on those bad days as you are today, are you?"

Sonny's expression was bleak. "No."

"Well," he went on, "the Assessment is sub-divided into four categories."

He paused, giving Jenny time to rub her husband's shoulder. She whispered her encouragement, "We need to know what it says, Hon, we have to know where we stand."

The doctor shifted his weight, keeping his expression neutral, stating the facts to help his patient understand. "The four categories are: 'Ability to understand and remember', 'Ability to sustain concentration', 'Social interaction', and 'Ability to adapt and tolerate stress'.

"Bottom line: on that day, in this doctor's opinion, you have 'significant limitations' in each of those areas." He met his patient's eyes, not looking away.

There was no response.

"What this basically means," he continued, "is that your status is unchanged. You should continue to be on disability."

Again he paused, but neither of them interrupted. "Of course, there may be grounds for re-evaluation."

“To re…re-test me? No thanks,” Sonny said. “I don’t want to go through that again.”

“Wait,” Jenny said, looking at the doctor. “Do you mean because of the neurostimulator?”

“Yes.” He nodded. “After a period of adjustment, getting used to the device, understanding how it effects for your quality of life, you might very well ask for a re-assessment.”

Jenny, realizing that her fingers were tired from massaging her concern into her husband’s shoulders, stepped around to face him. She pulled his hands, urging him to get up from the edge of the examining table. “You ready to go?”

The doctor placed his hand on the door knob. “We can revisit this whole issue in…let’s say six months. What do you say?”

Sonny nodded. “We’ll see how it goes.” He offered his hand to the doctor. “I appreciate it.”

“You appear to be quite alert today,” he observed, looking into his eyes as they shook hands, “these neurotransmitters have changed a lot of lives. Dr. Kinkaid is one of the best. Let’s make an appointment to see how you’re doing in, say, three months? See how you’re doing after a good period of adjustment?”

“Sounds fine,” Sonny answered.

“Funny…” He shook his head, taking Jenny’s hand as they walked to the appointment desk. “I don’t *feel* depressed.”

She squeezed his hand. “This will all work out in time, you’ll see.”

Chapter 28

"What is this, Grand Central Station?" Sonny said, hurrying to the ringing phone as they unlocked the front door. "Hello?"

The answering machine message started just as he answered. "Just a minute," he grumbled, waiting for the machine's message to complete.

"Sorry," he said.

"No problem," a soft southern female drawl answered. "Is this Sonny Jacobs?"

"Yeah?" He didn't recognize the voice.

"My name is Cindy Reed," she said. "I'm callin' for my husband, Joel?"

Sonny covered the receiver. "Joel's wife," he whispered; then moved his palm.

"Well, hello there, Cindy. Your husband's a ter…ter…he's a great singer!" He held the phone so that Jenny could hear both ends of the conversation. "My wife, Jenny, is here, too."

"Oh, sure. Hi, Jenny. Joel mentioned you, also.

"Nice t' meet ya. Joel sure likes y'all's music; he's memorized everything you've sent him. He says Sonny's songs are gonna *light up* Country Music! Joel really wants to be a part of it! He told me that singin' is very hard for you, Sonny. He's been prayin' for ya, hopin' you're feelin' better."

“Well, that’s very nice of him,” Sonny answered.

“Joel wanted me to let you know. He’s sorry he didn’t get to call you back.”

“Joel’s been very helpful,” Jenny told her. “There’s so much we don’t know about this business.”

“Anyways, he’s real sorry ’bout not callin’ and all. But you know how it is...” Cindy continued, “Joel’s stuck in Drippin’ Springs, Texas.”

She giggled. “Not stuck, really—it’s a *good* thing. He was supposed to do a backup guitar gig on Saturday for Johnny Gimble’s band? They’re havin’ a ‘Legends Of Texas Swing’ festival down there. Another band, Asleep At The Wheel? They had a picker get sick, with pneumonia.

“Looks like Joel’ll be there until Sunday, if the guy doesn’t get better? They want Joel to go with them on a west coast tour. That would last clear through Friday, the fifteenth!”

Sonny laughed, she had a funny way of phrasing her statements as questions. “I hope he’s...I hope he’s making a ton of money!”

Cindy laughed, too. “Lord knows we can sure use it!”

Jenny touched Sonny’s hand, gesturing to let her take the phone. “Hang on just a minute, Cindy,” she said into the handset.

Then to Sonny...”Girl talk, go take Fred for a walk or something.”

Sonny guessed he could wait a while longer before they listened to the message from the TV station. He went to get Fred’s leash.

****

“What’d you guys talk about?” Sonny asked a little later. Water was heating on the stove for a second cup of coffee.

“I asked her about Joel memorizing our songs. She said he’s serious, wants to talk to us about him recording some of our music.”

“Did she end all her sent...end her sent...did she talk in questions?” Sonny smiled. “I could listen to her talk all day.

“What I don’t understand is, how did Joel memorize our songs?”

“You mean, how did he *get* our songs? I copied him and some other people when I was sending them for ‘Lee-anne’ to approve for Gaylord.”

"Oh." Sonny dismissed further discussion about Joel. He was ready to hear about being on television. "You ready?" He pushed the button so they could review the recorded message from GAC.

Jenny jotted the caller's name and number on a yellow note pad as she listened.

"Mr. and Mrs. Jacobs, you don't know me…My name is Miranda Hendricks. I'm calling, let's see, it's about four, that would be five your time, Monday afternoon. I'm an associate producer with Great American Country television—GAC? I think we're Channel 54 over in your part of the state. Anyway, could you give me a call? I'll be available most of the evening. My cell number is: area code 615, 436-0987. That's Miranda Hendricks. Bye."

Jenny frowned at her coffee. "You forgot the sugar."

Sonny brought the container to the table and she stirred. "That's better.

"Last night you asked me if this TV network, GAC, has anything to do with the RMG Company. When we looked it up the other day, we didn't find any connection except they were carrying that awards show. So, I don't think this is something 'Lee-anne' set up."

"Let's call this…whatever her name is. This TV lady, and find out."

Jenny frowned again.

"What's wrong?"

She braced herself, trying not to let her feelings show. It had already been a tough day for her husband; the doctor's diagnosis of depression was very upsetting. The call from GAC TV was a beacon of hope.

This is just too weird! Jenny thought.

Yesterday afternoon Sonny had agreed—it was even his idea—not to perform anymore. Then he'd made that silly remark. 'But if someone asked me to sing just one song? I might do it.'

How providential, she thought, *somebody up there is watching over you, Sonny Jacobs!*

Jenny wasn't about to stand in the way of Providence. She brightened. "Nothing! Let's call and get you on TV!"

Since the call was long-distance, Jenny dialed using her cell phone.

"Ms. Hendricks, please. This is Jenny Jacobs calling."

In a moment…"This is Miranda. Thanks for returning my call, Jenny. Can I call you back in ten minutes? I'm in the middle of a production meeting at the moment." She hadn't been in Nashville long; there were still 'G's at the end of her words.

When she called back…"This is a different number, must be your cell," Miranda observed.

"Trying to save on long distance," Jenny answered. "My husband, Sonny, is here, listening in."

"Hello, Sonny." Mellow voice, Midwestern accent…Jenny remembered reading on their Web page that GAC's headquarters was in Colorado.

"I was at the Gaylord Center last Friday, doing background work for our interview with Clifton Jenson, and I saw Sonny perform. You were wonderful, by the way! I loved your song about the angel!"

"Thanks," Sonny said, wondering which song she meant.

"I had a whale of a time tracking you folks down," Miranda told them. "Finally, Clifton remembered that 'Jacob' was your performing name. He said your real name was Sonny Jacobs and that you were from Oak Ridge. Then I was able to look up your phone number."

Miranda paused a moment, getting her bearings. "Oh, I guess I should tell you who *I* am. I'm an associate producer for a show called 'Country Music Across America'. Have you seen it? Storme Warren and Vince Gill are the hosts, it's on several times a week, but the original taping is done on Thursdays, at nine."

Sonny and Jenny looked at each other; they'd never watched the GAC network but they'd certainly heard of Vince Gill.

Not hearing any response, Miranda continued with her explanation. "At any rate, I told Storme about you, Sonny, and we'd like to have you on the show with Clifton—Clifton's all for it, of course!"

"You want me to sing on TV?" Sonny croaked, having trouble getting out his question.

The woman laughed. "That's the idea."

"Well, sure!" Absently, he beeped his controller, adjusting for the excitement.

"Let me look at my notes," Miranda said.

"Oh, right…Clifton will be on first, talking about his tour, and we'll run a video of his newest single, 'It's Gotta Come From The Heart'. Then Storme will ask about his opening act. That would be you, Sonny."

"We're with you so far," Jenny said. She had switched to Pepsi while they waited for the return call. Now she tipped the glass with her elbow, spilling it.

"Oh, good Lord!" she muttered.

"Pardon me?"

"It's nothing," Jenny answered. "I just knocked over my soda. Go ahead, Clifton talks about Sonny, right?"

"By the way, do you have a video of that angel song? We could do some advance play."

Sonny laughed as his wife dabbed at the spilled beverage with a paper towel. "No, Miranda. We're just starting out. We can't afford a video."

The conversation went on for some time. Miranda explained that Storme liked to introduce new artists and wanted Sonny to sing the 'angel song', live. They determined that "Bev's Song" was the angel song Miranda had in mind.

That led to a conversation about the origin of the song. Jenny gave some of the background: Bev being on the list for a transplant, etc.

Miranda declared that the story would be a great introduction to Sonny's performance. He said that would be fine, but Jenny would have to do the talking.

The TV producer was flabbergasted when they told her they couldn't take any money for being on the show. "I'm sorry…" She laughed out loud. "But this is about the weirdest pre-show interview I've ever done.

"Storme is gonna love this. Sonny will sing, but Jenny has to do all the talking about the song…You don't have a video…You can send me an email attachment of the angel song, but you don't have any CDs for sale…And because Sonny is on disability, neither one of you can take any money for being on the show…Storme will *love* this!

"But we *have* to pay you for being on the show. It's only scale, but still…

"How about we donate the money to your church?"

"Our youth group takes a mission trip to…"

"They go to the Cherokee reservation in North Carolina." Jenny finished Sonny's sentence for him.

"Yeah, every summer," Sonny said. "You can make the check out to them."

They talked about what time to arrive for the taping: "The crew will want to run through everything with you and Clifton beginning at about four o'clock." Miranda gave Jenny the address of the recording studio, in Nashville.

"We'll see you there," Jenny said as Miranda hung up.

She turned to her husband. "So, you think this will be alright, huh? One song won't make you sick?"

"Nah." He grinned. "One song shouldn't be too bad. Let's call…call Doug, and Jim, and the you…youth pastor."

"And my mom…" Jenny was getting into it. "And Lisa and Blake, and we'll email Joel and John and Toni. And we've got to call Jerry in Harriman, and…"

Chapter 29

Stan Hamilton was pale. Mary, his wife, didn't look like she was holding up very well, either. They both had that gaunt, skin-clinging-to-facial-bones look that comes with sudden terrible stress. *This is only the beginning,* Sonny thought to himself.

"Long time no see," Sonny said. "What's it been? Two seasons ago?"

"Yeah," Stan answered, his voice barely above a whisper. "Back when you got sick. I should have called and checked on you, but…"

"Remember that best-ball tournament out at Centennial?" Sonny interrupted, changing the subject. "I think we used my ball about three…three times in eighteen holes. You couldn't miss that day."

They talked—actually Sonny did the talking, Stan mostly listened to his stories—about golf and coaching. They talked about Todd, who had been Sonny's starting shortstop for three years in the late '90s. They talked about the couples' two younger children, Mike and Gertrude. Sonny still laughed when he said her name; how did they ever come up with 'Gertrude'?

Stan rubbed the top of his nearly-bald head. "My hair's coming out by the handful," he told Sonny.

"It'll grow back. That reminds me, I brought a ball…ball cap for you. It's out in the car. You can show your…colors when you go for treatments.

"Hey, remember that pick…pick-off play we used to beat West in the Regionals? You taught Jason to turn and walk away with his back…with his back to the base, then count two and Bam! We got' em!" He laughed at the memory. "They had two guys on and we were only up one run. We got all the way to…"

"That was the year you guys went to the District finals," Mary said.

Sonny reminisced a while longer about teams and players they had coached.

"Are you still writing songs?" Mary asked.

Sonny glanced at Stan's guitar, a 12-string acoustic on its stand, there in the corner of the den. "What about you?" He looked at his friend. "You still pick a little, don't you?"

Stan had studied classical guitar in college; his and Sonny's tastes in music were light years apart. "Our middle son, Mike, is better at it than I am," Stan answered softly. "I still strum a little, sometimes when I can't sleep at night." He lay back on his pillow, on the couch.

"Oh, hey, I almost forgot!" Sonny brightened. "I'm gonna be on TV!"

They talked about Tootsies and the Gaylord Center and GAC.

"Karen Norton was telling us about the Gaylord show," Mary told him, "she said you were great!"

Sonny gave his 'Aw Shucks' shrug. "Anyway, to answer your question, I *am* wor…working on a song. Why do you ask?"

"We thought," Mary began, "well, the kids and I were talking and…"

Sonny smiled. "Maybe I could do a song Sunday. I could see if…"

"Dr. Martin?" Mary prompted.

"Yeah, our illustrious pastor, Dr. Mike Martin. He's a nice guy isn't he? He's brought a bunch of new fam…families into the congregation.

"Jenny and I have been kinda ab…absent from church for a while, but we're getting back into it. Everyone's been so nice—it's like we never stopped.

"Anyway, I could call and see if…"

"Dr. Martin…"

"Yeah, if he would let me do a 'special music' number. Want me to do it in the morning service or evening?" *Hope I can come up with something,* Sonny thought, *this one is gonna have to come quick*!

"Evening would be nice," Stan whispered.

"Tell you what," he told them, "I'll pr…pray about it. Something will come."

On his way home, Sonny was nearly in tears. *Here I am feeling sorry for myself and Stan is…*He couldn't finish the thought. A picture leaped into his mind. His friend, strumming his guitar, late at night.

Been there, done that, he thought. Then the lyrics and melody started to come to him for Stan's song.

Sittin' up at two AM
my old twelve-string and me
Pickin' out a favorite hymn
waitin' on the urge to sleep

"Thank you, Lord," Sonny murmured aloud. He sang the new verse, over and over, as he drove across town, back home.

****

Despite the fact that he had a song to write and yard work to do, now that spring was finally here, Sonny spent most of the day resting. "I'm beginning to get an understanding," he told Jenny, tapping his controller on the nightstand. "If I don't overdo, if I rest some every day…and don't get too excited or work too long out in the yard or something…

"I think the so-called bad…bad days might not be quite so bad." He beeped his controller. "Truth is, though, I just can't get his thing ad…ad…set right on these days. I guess it's like…what's her name?"

"Ginny," Jenny interjected.

"Yeah, it's like Ginny said, 'Bad…bad days will still be bad'."

Sonny managed a short walk with Fred in the early afternoon, but wasn't able to make it to the Wednesday evening church service.

Jenny was determined to go.

"If you see Mary," Sonny said, "tell her I'm working on Stan's song. Oh, and we need to ask…"

"I'll ask Dr. Martin about a 'special music' time for the Sunday evening service," Jenny assured him. "You get your rest. Like you said, if you don't get too excited, maybe today will be the only 'bad' day this time."

Chapter 30

"When we were first introduced," Clifton Jenson was telling Storme Warren, the host of GAC's talk show, "it was 'Jacob'. I think there was some confusion."

The red light was glowing on the camera facing Clifton; they were 'live' on Country Music Across America.

"It was one of those, what-you-heard-isn't-what-I-said things…" Jenny started to explain, and then shook her head. "Doesn't matter, Jacobs is our last name."

"In any case," Storme said, "welcome to you both, Sonny and Jenny Jacobs."

Storme Warren was a young guy. No big cowboy hat, no shoulder-length hairstyle, he looked and talked more like the host of a fishing show. He was dressed in a golf shirt and wash pants; there was only a trace of Country in his accent. "I read Peter Poindexter's review of your opening show, Sonny. One of our producers was actually there to hear you at the Gaylord Center. I understand your songs are something special. Tell us about the angel song."

Neither Sonny nor Jenny was nervous. Miranda had done a good job of introducing everyone, making them feel at ease. The small studio audience—there were maybe 50 people—seemed friendly and supportive.

The set wasn't arranged like Leno's or Letterman's. Instead, they were sitting in a semicircle of high stools; there were three cameras, two were set up to look over their shoulders, rather than challenging them head-on. Behind them was a huge projection screen. At the moment their backdrop was a picturesque scene of two horses grazing in a green pasture.

Sonny had the Stratocaster on his lap; he placed his fingers on its neck, forming a 'C' chord. "It's called 'Bev's Song'," he answered the host's prompt, "but I'd ra…rather not say what the song's about."

Jenny had to react quickly! She and Miranda had talked about this—the story behind the song was supposed to be used as an introduction. Now, Sonny was balking.

"Our songs are stories, really, Storme." Jenny hurried to pick up her husband's thought as another camera found her. "Stories about angels and miracles. In this case the story is about one of my very best friends, a woman named Beverly. We called her Bev.

"But what I *hope*." She paused and looked at her husband. "What *we* hope, is that every person who hears this song will have their own version, see their own story. We decided a long time ago that a song should be about whatever the *listener* wants it to be."

The camera focused on Jenny as she spoke, running her fingers through the part in the middle of her thick, shimmering auburn hair.

If she sang, Storme thought to himself, watching her, *she'd bring the house down!* He rolled his shoulders, off-camera, bringing himself back to reality.

"That's an interesting perspective, Jenny," he said to the camera, "but it really doesn't answer my question."

He turned back to Sonny, wanting a better answer—something mystical maybe, or supernatural. "Do you see angels when you write your songs?"

As one of the flanking cameras focused on Sonny, his expression darkened.

Suddenly he was nauseous. He felt an all-too-familiar burning in his neck, a pounding in the joints of his shoulders! Jenny was supposed to handle the questions!

Jenny saw a flare-up coming—Sonny was about to get angry—that was the last thing they needed!

"Now, Storme..." She rescued her husband, bringing the red light of the camera back to herself with another dazzling smile. "It's not polite to put your guests on the spot. Sonny's a wonderful storyteller! Why don't you give him a chance to answer your questions in his own way, with our song?" She watched Sonny as she spoke; he calmed down.

Storme shrugged, directly into the camera. *Well, I tried,* his body language told the viewing audience.

Then aloud..."What say we take a break? When we come back, we'll give Sonny a chance to do his 'storytelling'. We'll be right back."

****

Sonny reached into his pocket and pulled out his controller. He'd have to make two sets of adjustments: first to accommodate the sudden stress caused by Storme's questions, then he would make the adjustments required for him to play and sing. Fortunately, this was scheduled to be a three-minute commercial break.

Jenny walked over to rub his neck. "You're going to knock 'em dead, Hon!" she whispered, as he made his adjustments, "just relax a minute."

"Thirty seconds..." an off-camera voice announced as Sonny felt the 'funny-bone' tingling in his arms and fingers. He winked at Jenny as she went back to her seat.

Everyone had been prompted ahead of time; they knew what to expect. "The camera won't just stay on you," Miranda had told Sonny, "we'll be looking at Jenny, Clifton and Storme, as well as panning around the audience."

Getting there early had given the technicians time to work up some background scenes to complement the song; there were film clips of clouds in a high sky, an antique oval-shaped mirror in a huge empty room, and a wide peaceful blue-green river.

When the red light came on, Sonny gave a tug at his ball cap and began fingering a long, slow 'C'-chord, leaning forward into the microphone.

Lord, we sure could use a miracle today

Again, the words weren't just an opening line; they were a prayer. Then he began stroking the Fender guitar in earnest, the praying man becoming a storyteller.

I wasn't list'ning for angels singing when I woke up today
And I stopped looking for miracles somewhere along the way…

The background shifts were expertly timed. Camera shots of the crowd showed each person following along with the song's lyric, caught up in the rhythm of his playing.

Storme was surprised by his own emotions as the song's story unfolded. Sonny sang the final verse, about a single drop of rain falling into the river, washing away his reflection, letting him see an angel. One of the side-view cameras caught the glistening in Storme's eyes.

The song ended as it began, with a prayer.

Lord, we sure could use a miracle today

When he finished, Sonny pushed the bill of his cap up, away from his forehead. He smiled, looking at their host.

Storme Warren didn't try to cover-up his feelings. "You know," he said, reaching for Jenny's hand—she was sitting on the stool to his left.

"You were right, Jenny. I didn't know Bev, but I know a girl named Sandy." He looked into the camera again. "Sandy," he said, his voice breaking, "I know you're watching, Baby, and I know you saw the angel in that river. I love you, Sandy…"

And the red light went off as they cut to a commercial.

****

When the break was over, a more composed host asked Sonny where he would be appearing next. "We don't have anything definite right now," Sonny answered.

The camera over Clifton's shoulder caught Jenny's surprise at his answer. She started to say that he wouldn't *be* performing any more, but then thought better of it. "We're still pretty new at all this, Storme," she murmured.

The camera angle changed back to Storme. "Maybe a video, sometime soon? I know our viewers would love to see that angel story on a video!"

Jenny smiled. "Thanks so much, Storme, for giving us a chance to let people hear our music."

Storme looked into the lens. "Vince, Buddy, you picked a bad time to be out on location. This has been *some* show!" He turned back to his guests. "That was one fine song, Sonny. And Jenny, thanks so much for being here, we'd love to have you both on again."

Storme gestured toward Clifton. "We owe it all to you, Clifton, for introducing us. And good luck on the rest of your national tour.

"Goodnight folks," Storme said into the camera again. "And God bless."

Chapter 31

The phone rang, for maybe the tenth time, just after lunch on Friday. "Hello, may I speak to Coach Jacobs, please?" It was a young man's voice.

"Sonny," Jenny called, "it's for you."

"Hello?" Sonny's tone was bright—today was a great day!

His stimulator was set at less than 2.5—on a day after performing—singing just one song hadn't bothered him at all! People had been calling all morning to compliment them on their TV appearance.

"This is Sonny!" he said into the receiver.

"Hello Coach, this is Todd Hamilton. Do you remember me?"

"Sure I do, Todd," he replied. "Todd Hamilton," Sonny mouthed to Jenny, then back into the receiver, "One of my best…best infielders ever! How's your dad doing? I was going to…"

"Not so well, Coach. Mom said you were working on a song for him, maybe going to sing it at the Sunday evening service?"

Todd's tone was somber; Sonny turned his own enthusiasm down a couple of notches. "You can tell your mother I'm al…almost done. I could come by and play it for you guys ahead of time if you'd like."

"Dad's back in the hospital, Coach. The doctors told Mom to let Grandma and Dad's brothers know that it's looking really bad."

"Oh Lord, Todd, I am so sorry to hear that. Is there anything Jenny and I can do?

"We could…Anything at all, Todd, just let us know if there's anything." Jenny caught his eye; he raised his palm. There was nothing to say until after he got off the phone.

"Like I said, Coach," Stan's eldest son said, "Mom wanted me to let you know. So you wouldn't have to hurry and finish that song. I don't think any of us will be able to…"

"I understand perfectly, Todd. You and your mom have more important things on your mind. Are they…are they allowing visitors?"

"No, Sir, only immediate family in the ICU. Listen," the young man said, sniffing back his tears. "I have to go. Mom asked me to call."

"Tell your dad we'll be pray…praying for him, Todd. Everyone at church and all the kids he's coached and tau…taught over the years, I'm sure we'll all be praying for your dad!"

"Thanks, Coach." Todd said, and he hung up.

"Stan's back in the hospital," Sonny told Jenny, "in ICU. They've called in his family, it doesn't look good."

"I heard you say we'd be praying for him," Jenny said, taking both his hands in hers, "now's a good time."

They bowed their heads, together there at the kitchen table, and prayed.

****

"You know, we ought to get away," Sonny said later that afternoon. His shoulders were stiff, he felt nauseous. He wrinkled his forehead as he reached for his controller. "Wait, I need to adjust this."

I'm still not completely used to what this thing can do for me, he thought as he upped the amperage one tenth at a time. He walked out of the room, on his way to the back porch, sensing relief as he walked.

Jenny followed him outside. "This *is* getting away," she told her husband as she sat in a wicker chair, "right here on our own porch."

Three crabapple trees, evenly spaced at the south end of their back yard, were starting to bloom a bright pink. The two dogwoods next to the fence had buds; one would be a pale pink, the other a silvery white. "Just look at all this; right here in our back yard."

"I wonder why Aneda's dogwoods bloom before ours? I guess they're older," Sonny asked and answered his own question.

The next-door-neighbor's three mature dogwoods were already in full bloom. "It *is* pretty back here this time of year. I was talking about getting away from, you know, the phone and email." He paused, smiling as he realized that the neurostimulator adjustment had done its job, his nausea was gone. "I used to go days without ever talking to anyone. It seems like life is speeding up, now. Do you know what I mean?"

"I do," she answered, reaching to scratch behind Fred's ears. "We don't like all this activity, do we, Freddy? We're used to having everything nice and quiet."

She looked up at Sonny. "In a way, though, it's like we're getting our life back. Maybe your days of teaching and coaching are done, Sonny, but we can still lead a busy, productive life. Going to ballgames, having people over sometimes…

"Working on the song for Stan and your other new one, 'Why Doesn't He Sing'—maybe that's what you're supposed to be doing with your life now. Maybe you should be devoting your time and energy to *writing* music."

"That's too bad about Stan," Sonny said, distracted. "Todd sounded pretty torn…torn up, just now."

"At least you got to brighten his day yesterday, Hon, you're a good friend. What did you guys talk about?"

"I did most of the talking, he was very weak. We talked about the days we coach…coached together. Stuff like that."

"You haven't asked me to listen to Stan's song, like you usually do when you start a new one."

"It's too sad. I can't come up with anything for the chorus except 'Tell her there's an angel standing by'."

"Well, it'll come to you." Jenny wanted to get back to their discussion. "So what do you think? About the music business, I mean. If we *do* figure out a way to get your songs published, we're going to be spending a lot of time on the phone and on the computer, too. That seems to be how things are done in the music business."

"Maybe so…I'm not much on the phone, though, I never did like talk…talking without being face-to-face.

"Anyway," he changed gears. "Doing just one…just one song like that, like I did last night, it didn't seem so bad. Maybe I…"

Jenny's expression changed abruptly. She was ready to do battle.

"Oh no you don't, Sonny Jacobs! We've already settled that. You promised, no more performing!"

"But I feel fine today. Maybe if I just…if I do one song; every once in a while?"

"I doubt there will be much opportunity for single song performances. But if something like that comes along, once in a while…" She paused, seeing his face brighten. "But we still need to find someone *else* to perform your songs, Sonny. Someone who has the energy it takes to do tours like Clifton is doing. He said he'd be in twenty-five different cities over the next two months. That's a lot of traveling!"

"Yeah," he admitted, "imagine how much turned-up amperage it would take to shoot a video or record enough songs for a whole CD album. I'd be completely off the wall. I guess writing, and maybe helping some other singer understand how our songs should sound—that would be pretty cool!"

Sonny stood up, leaning on the porch railing. "My horseshoe pits are full of weeds; I need some new sand."

Jenny joined him at the railing. "I want you to dig me a garden patch over in that corner for my tomatoes." She pointed to the far northeast corner of the back yard. "The sun shines there, even late in the afternoon when the house shadow covers most of the yard."

"Okay, I can do that."

As Sonny sat back down, Fred ambled two steps over to get attention from his master. "What do you think, Pal?" he asked his dog as he rolled over to let Sonny pet his belly. "Maybe *you* could go on the road and sing our songs."

Fred yawned and stared at Sonny with lazy brown eyes. "Well, maybe not," Sonny said.

"I know who I *wish* could do it," Jenny said, sitting, too. She reached to touch his elbow, catching his attention.

"Who?"

"Joel Reed."

"Joel?" Sonny frowned.

"Yes, Joel." She saw his expression. "Why, what do you think?"

"We don't sing anything alike. My voice is a lot deep…deeper than his."

Sensing that Joel singing his songs was something that Jenny wanted to consider, he reflected a moment. "You said yourself, Babe, when he was singing those Glen…Glen Campbell songs. It's no big deal to sound like someone else.

"Hey, remember, even Toni…even Toni said she and Joel were *what*?"

"She said they were a couple of hacks. But I don't think she meant it in a bad way. She meant there was lots of competition."

Jenny backtracked. "Why do you think Joel should sound like you, with a deeper voice? When he sang his Claude Monet song, he sang it from his heart. I thought it was really good."

"You thought that song was good?"

"Not the song. The way he sang it. He really believed in what the song had to say; you could tell it meant a lot to him. What did they call it, a 'hook'? Joel was looking for his hook."

"I can't picture Joel in a baseball cap." Sonny grinned.

Jenny laughed. "Neither can I, Sonny."

He was afraid she missed his point. "But Joel and Toni said that my appearance—the ball cap and all—was part of my…hook. See what I mean?"

"It wouldn't be part of Joel's hook, Hon."

She gave some thought to his argument. He was right; the cowboy look didn't seem like a good fit for their music. "But who knows, maybe he wouldn't wear his cowboy hat and that big belt buckle, either, if he sang our songs. He might change his look to something else entirely.

"I think the main thing is that he loves our music, he believes in our songs!"

"His wife, what's her name?"

"Cindy," Jenny answered.

"Yeah, Cindy. Cindy *did* say he had mem…memorized some of our stuff. Do you think that's true?"

Jenny nodded. "That's why I wanted to talk to her some more when she called. I asked her if she thought our music was really special to him or if he was just trying to…I don't know."

She shook her head. "But Cindy said Joel is absolutely committed to trying to get us to let him be…what did she call it? 'Part'—she said Joel wanted to be 'part of our music'.

"I think we should get together with him, see how he feels. Let him record a couple of songs if he wants to."

"Fine with me. He's so busy, though. When can we get together?"

"We're in no hurry, are we?"

"No, that's true. You're right, let's give him a chance.

"And you're right, too, Jen, about be…believing. If he really *believes* in our music…that would make a big difference."

Chapter 32

"I thought Vince Gill was supposed to be one of the hosts on your TV show," Doug said at the beginning of Sunday school class. "Whoever heard of 'Stormy Warning'? That's a really dumb name."

The class was held in the east corner on the second floor, there was more sunlight in that classroom than any other. The seven men, all dressed in light warm-weather suits, were seated in metal folding chairs around a collapsible table, lesson books open.

They had just come from the 'at-large' session, where all the adults, men and women, met for announcements and prayer requests. Stan Hamilton had been moved from ICU to a regular room but was still much in need of everyone's prayers. Several others were lifted up for special prayer consideration; Sonny and Jenny didn't recognize two of the names. Sonny raised his hand and stood to thank everyone for their prayers over the past months. "As most of you know," he told them, "I'm doing quite a bit better now that I've got my implant."

Don Raymond, an affable retired physicist and the senior men's class leader, figured there wouldn't be much time devoted to the planned lesson this morning, Joshua 1:9 'For the Lord thy God is with thee withersoever thou goest'.

He didn't mind; it was good to have Sonny back with them.

Sonny grinned in response to Doug's ribbing. "I don't think his last name is 'Warning', they said Vince Gill was…'on location' or something like that."

"So," Jim asked, "you weren't sick Saturday, after singing?"

"Nah, it was only one…only one song," Sonny said.

Don had watched the show; everyone in the class had heard about it in advance. "I sure liked your song! You sang it before at church, I think, but not like that. Doug was saying you do something with your implant controller. You *did* look a bit stressed when you were singing."

"He tried to put…to put me on the spot." Sonny shook his head. "Asking whether I saw angels. Jenny had to rescue me."

"I've got a question," Tom Hazelton said. Tom was the youngest member of the group, in his late 40's. An accountant by trade, Tom took the 'Doubting Thomas' point of view in every class discussion. He loved to stir things up.

Sonny rolled his eyes. "Go ahead."

Hazelton made a show of pulling a pen from the pocket protector in his shirt, tapping the point on his ever-present steno pad. Rather than look Sonny in the eye, he scribbled a large question mark on his pad.

"I was talking with my wife, Sarah. I asked her if she remembered. Neither of us could recall, specifically, about the song you sang Thursday evening, but we were *both* under the impression that *you* wrote all the songs you sing."

"And…" Sonny prompted.

"And," Tom mimicked, avoiding Sonny's glare. "On that TV show, you both kept saying 'our'…'our songs'."

"Oh." Sonny inhaled slowly, to maintain his composure. "Well, they are…they are our songs, Jenny's and mine. All of them are ours."

"Technically," Doug interjected, "they're Jenny's songs, aren't they, Sonny?" Rachel had told him all about Jerry Hinkle's copyright idea. "Her name is on the copyrights. That way, if someone records one of your songs, Jenny gets the commission or whatever it's called—keeps you out of trouble with your disability payments."

Sonny nodded, and then looked at Tom. That would be good fodder for Doubting Thomas.

"Technically…" Hazelton drew the word out, printing a dollar sign next to the question mark on his steno pad. "It's kinda questionable to stretch the truth when your songs are about angels and miracles, don't you think?"

“Make your point,” Sonny said flatly.

“Well, really, Jenny had nothing to do with the composing of any of your songs, did she?” Tom Hazelton looked over at Don, the group leader, for support.

Don didn’t mind being pulled into Hazelton’s argument, he could nit pick with the best of them. “Sarah doesn’t have a job outside the home, does she, Tom?”

Doubting Tomas was perplexed by the question. “As everybody at this table knows…” He was indignant. “Sarah and I have five school-age children. She’s a stay-at-home mother.”

Jim saw where Don was going; he couldn’t help but jump in. “Does Sarah ever say ‘our house’, Tom? Or maybe, ‘our car’?”

Doug kicked Jim under the table—he flinched! Everyone in the room laughed, except Tom.

“Sorry,” Jim said to Hazelton. “But you see the point, don’t you? Sonny and Jenny both own those songs in the same way that you and Sarah, and your kids for that matter, own your home.”

Now Don Raymond came to Hazelton’s rescue. “Let’s turn our attention to the Old Testament, shall we, gentlemen? Tom, why don’t you read our scripture for today, Joshua one:nine.”

Chapter 33

On Monday there was yet another email from Lynne at RMG.

From: lynne@SouthernChristian.com
Date: Monday, April 11, 2005, 10:08 AM
To: Sonnyandjen@bellsouth.net
Subject: Congrats!

Dear Jenny and Sonny,

I saw you on GAC's Country Music Across America! It was wonderful!

I know you're very busy, but when you have time, please give me a call!

Mr. Randall is VERY interested in talking with you both about PUBLISHING YOUR SONGS!!

Thanks!

Lynne Lewis, RMG, 615-322-8198—ext.12

"She's per…persistent, if nothing else," Sonny said, reading over Jenny's shoulder. He was just back from an early-evening walk with Fred; they'd made the complete 7-mile trek along Melton Lake Trail. "How many messages has she sent since last Thursday?"

"One every morning, one every afternoon," Jenny answered.

"Are you going to mail her back?"

"As soon as the temperature in Hades drops about one hundred degrees," she answered. She pointed to the computer screen. "But that's not why I wanted you to come in here. We've got another message."

She brought up an email from Toni, Joel's singing partner at Tootsies.

From: Toniclarkston@Countryconnections.com
Date: Monday, April 11, 2005, 3:12 PM
To: Sonnyandjen@bellsouth.net
Cc: Joel@joelReed.com,
JohnTyler@tootsies.net
Subject: You're in the news!

Dear Jenny and Sonny,

Saw you on GAC! I told you we'd see you on TV someday!

Joel's been out of town with Asleep At The Wheel. Great gig! Anyway, I didn't know about you singing on Country Music Across America. I just happened to be watching a rerun late Sunday night. Love that angel song!

We're still the 'house band' at Tootsies for a couple more weeks. It's nice to have a steady income.

I HAVE GREAT NEWS!!!!!

CeeCee Winans wants you to open for her at Dollywood!

Her publicist, Harold Meyers, should call either today or tomorrow. She definitely wants "Bev's Song" to be one of the songs you do.

Anyway, I'm copying John on this to remind him that I'll need Saturday afternoon off to come and see the show. Oh, almost forgot. The Dollywood show is at 2:00 on Saturday, the 16th. I wouldn't miss it!

Toni

"Wow!" Sonny said. "Did that Harold guy call yet?"

"Not yet," Jenny answered; her voice was flat.

"Dollywood!" he whooped, raising his hands in the air.

Raising his arms caused his neurostimulator to give him a jolt! "Ouch!" he grunted, and then continued celebrating, "Dollywood, Jenny! Sonny Jacobs—opening for CeeCee Winans!"

Jenny didn't respond.

Sonny noticed. "Hey! What's with you, Babe? Aren't you excited? Dollywood, Babe, with a first-class Gospel Music act!"

When she looked away he stopped celebrating. "Oh…" he said.

"Yes, 'Oh' is right." Jenny said.

"Well, maybe…maybe it will be just one or two songs."

She shook her head. "Not likely. Opening for a big act, they'll want at least five songs. We both know what that would do to you."

"Jenny, come on…You're right; this *is* a big act! This is CeeCee Winans we're talking about!"

She let out a nervous laugh. "Until a few days ago, you'd never heard of CeeCee. Can you name even one of her songs?"

"That's not the point, Jen!" Sonny slammed his palm on the computer desk. "Do you want to get *your* music published or not?"

Jenny stood up. "*My* music?"

He dropped his eyes. "Sorry, that was out of line."

"You bet it was. Sonny, this goes all the way back to before you got the power pack implanted.

"Don't you remember? Back then, I said it was dangerous—dangerous music! And you know what? I was right! How long do you think you can go on abusing that device? How many more performances before your body shuts down for good?"

His eyes grew wide. He had been angry, but now she was scaring him! "Did one of the doc…doctors say something? Did they tell you something bad about…"

She reached to touch his face, wanting to reassure him. "No, it's not like that…"

He pushed her hand away. "Then what is it? Are you so set…so set against this that you'll use scare tactics?"

"Scare tactics? Is that what you think—that I'm trying to *scare* you?"

He backed away a step, trying to get his bearings. "I just meant…"

She dropped her hand and turned to walk out of the room. "It's *me* who's scared, Sonny. I'm scared to death."

She stopped in the doorway and turned back to him. Her voice was only a whisper. "You know what, Sonny? I'm not going to fight you any more. Just go ahead… When that guy calls, tell him you'll sing, tell him you'll sing a hundred songs if you want to…"

Jenny walked out of the room and Sonny heard the front door close as she left. He watched her back the car out of the carport and drive away.

Chapter 34

Sonny grinned at Jenny. "All set?"

Jenny smiled back at him. "Sure, Hon. It's going to be wonderful!"

Her smile was genuine. She was here and she would be supportive. What else could she do? Her husband was putting himself in great jeopardy but he was determined to go ahead with it—he was living his dream!

She had wrestled with herself the night of their fight; much like the Biblical Jacob had wrestled with the Angel of God. *I will not let you go until you bless me.*

For nearly two years Jenny had watched helplessly at her husband's anguish, watched his hope fade into despair. Finally, medical science had given back his life.

But Providence was capricious.

If Sonny would go one step beyond what medical science had given him, one step beyond reason…there was a new promise. The promise of a fulfilling life—hope, after so much misery!

When her wrestling was finished that night, Jenny's answer was clear. She had to be part of Sonny's hope!

She had to be here—she had to be right beside him.

****

Doug and Rachel had insisted that the two couples ride along in their van for the 60-mile trip to Dollywood in Pigeon Forge, Sonny and Jenny, Jim and Karen.

The billboard in front of the Showstreet Palace, across from the main entrance at Dollywood read:

CeeCee Winans in Concert
Special guest appearance by Sonny Jacobs

"Now you've made the Big Time." Jim Norton was carrying John Tyler's Fender guitar for Sonny. "And it even says 'Sonny' this time, no more 'Jacob'!"

"We've got awhile before the show," Rachel said as Jenny used their complimentary tickets for admission to the park. "We might as well go see the sights."

"You guys go ahead," Jenny told them, "we'd better get our bearings, find out how things are set up in there." She pointed up the steps to the theatre entrance.

"Yeah, have a good time," Sonny said, "we'll see you after the show!"

Jim handed the guitar case to Sonny. "Break a leg, man. Isn't what they say?"

"You bet!" Sonny was still grinning.

****

The backstage area of the Showstreet Palace was nicely laid out, providing well-appointed soundproof dressing rooms for the performers. They met briefly with the stage director and then went to their assigned room. CeeCee herself would not arrive until much closer to her 3:15 appearance time; they would meet her after the show.

"They said I can sit right off to the side, in the wings," Jenny told him.

"Good, I'll look over at you if I forget the lyrics." Sonny laughed, glancing at the clock. "Still about twenty minutes," he said, taking a long swallow of Coke.

There was a quick knock as the door rushed open. In bounced John Tyler, Toni Clarkson and Joel Reed. All three were bubbling over with excitement!

"Hey, how's everybody?" John said, rushing to hug Jenny, then to shake Sonny's hand.

Toni was next in line, hugging both Jenny and Sonny. "This is it! Y'all ready?"

Joel was initially more reserved, warily approaching Jenny for his turn to hug, but she pulled him close. "Joel, it's wonderful to see you!" she exclaimed, including all their guests in her greeting, "…it's wonderful to see *all* of you!"

Sonny returned the hugs and handshakes with enthusiasm. He tucked in his shirt and retrieved his ball cap from the arm of the couch. "All set!" he said, looking into the mirror of the makeup table. "What do you guys think?"

"Push your hat back on your forehead." Toni giggled. "You're not supposed to pull it down until you get ready to sing."

"This is some…'gig' you got us, Toni!"

"It took a while, but CeeCee finally came around—worked out good being here at Dollywood." She plopped down on the couch. "Is this a great setup, or what?"

"We really do appreciate it, Toni," Jenny added, smiling at her.

Sonny bent down to pull the Stratocaster from its case, moving to the couch to strum a 'C' chord. He'd tuned and re-tuned it every day since hearing that he was going to perform at Dollywood. "I can't go wrong with an instrument like this." He smiled at John, and then turned his attention to Joel. "When did you get back?"

"I flew into Knoxville this morning, instead of Nashville. I rented a car to get here; Cindy and my daughter, Kasi, are meeting me."

"That's nice," Jenny said. "We can get together after the show. It will be great to meet your family!" She was getting caught up in their friends' enthusiasm. "Cindy and I talked on the phone. She sounds like a really nice person."

"Look for all of us in the 'Front Row'." John gave a poor imitation of Bob Uecker. "Toni got us good seats."

Toni looked at her watch. "We'd better let you get ready." She gave Sonny a final hug. "Good luck!"

****

Jenny could hear the audience from her seat on a stool in the wings. Something astonishing happened. When Sonny spoke the first line of his song—

Lord, we sure could use a miracle today

—hundreds of people in the audience whispered it with him!

Sonny had no CDs for sale and there was certainly no video, but somehow people knew that first line! *Amazing,* Jenny shook her head as Sonny picked up with the first verse, *absolutely amazing*!

I wasn't list'ning for angels singing when I woke up today
And I stopped looking for miracles somewhere along the way…

The song was wonderfully received. She heard the whispering again, at the last line of the song, the same single-line prayer.

Lord, we sure could use a miracle today

The applause was voluble and heartfelt. Sonny tilted his cap back, giving them his 'Aw Shucks' smile. In another moment he reset his cap and started the song about his friend, Wilfred.

It's me again Lord, Prayin' for a friend
We need your help Lord, we need your guiding hand…

Again, the audience responded! *More praying! More angels!* Their applause was telling Sonny.

And again, he made no introductions for his next song. He was aware of Jenny in his peripheral vision. He'd make her proud!

He played the opening minor-key chords to "Angel With The Light In His Eyes," then began to sing.

I pulled in the drive, under stormy skies
I was tired and the hour was late…

Suddenly, there was a loud screech from Sonny's guitar. The audiencc saw him fall from the stool!

They watched in alarm as Sonny flung the Stratocaster guitar away from his body—it went skittering across the floor! His arms began to convulse, flying first above his head, and then jerking at his sides!

He struggled to his knees! "Ungh!" Sonny cried out, "Ungh!"

Then a woman was there—a tall woman with her red hair tied in a severe bun behind her head. The woman reached into Sonny's pocket. The audience saw her place the device from his pocket—whatever it was—next to the singer's shoulder. They heard several faint beeps!

As suddenly as they had begun, Sonny's convulsions stopped.

He sat very still for a long moment, looking at the woman. "That's his wife, Jenny!" someone said.

In another moment Sonny was standing. Holding onto his wife's arm for support, he strode over to retrieve his guitar. Together, they walked to the microphone.

"I'll be okay…" Sonny said. He and his wife exited the stage.

Chapter 35

CeeCee Winans was scheduled for a costume change between sets.

The conductor for her orchestra stepped to a microphone. "Ladies and Gentlemen," he said, "CeeCee wanted to assure everyone that Sonny Jacobs is doing alright.

"While we've got a short break, CeeCee suggested that Sonny come out and do the final song of his act." He turned to his right. "Ladies and Gentlemen, meet Jenny Jacobs."

"Hello everyone, sorry about the scare we put you through." Jenny held her chin up high as she spoke into the microphone. "As some of you may know, there are times when singing is very hard for Sonny."

A hush came over the audience. A short, square-chinned man, dressed in a blue sports coat, over a button-down white shirt with casual khaki slacks, was bringing a guitar and a high stool out onto the stage. Beside him was the storyteller—Sonny Jacobs.

Sonny came to sit on a stool directly behind his wife, reaching to touch her shoulder. He did not have his guitar with him.

Jenny pressed on with her explanation, "A very good friend of ours, Mr. Joel Reed, is going to help us out a little with this song. It's called 'Rainbows to Paint'."

She turned away from the audience, then decided to make the introductions again as Joel pulled his stool into place next to Sonny. "Joel Reed," Jenny said into the microphone, "and Sonny Jacobs. 'Rainbows To Paint'."

Joel played the introductory chords, a 'D' progression, just as he had memorized from the email attachments Jenny had sent so long ago.

It was Joel Reed who painted the picture with his guitar and his voice: a tiny chapel, a weary traveler, and a welcoming older gentleman, over in the corner.

He was sittin' in a corner
when I came into the room
Playin' chords and singin'
an unfamiliar tune

As I sat down to listen
each word he sang rang true
All the hurt my heart was feelin'
seemed like he knew

Sonny turned his face toward Joel, smiling and encouraging him as he started the second verse.

He sang about an angel
standin' oh, so near
Whisperin' every word
that my heart needed to hear

And when the song had ended
he bowed his head to pray
He said thank you for the music, Lord
guess we'll call it a day

It was time for the chorus. Sonny turned his face back to his microphone. He was going to sing the harmony part in his regular, unaltered voice; Sonny had not upped the amperage on his neurotransmitter.

Joel continued, starting the chorus:

Then he put away his guitar, in a ragged old case
And I started walkin' toward him, just to tell him thanks

This was where Sonny came in. He sang the two lines, his deep baritone voice in perfect accord with Joel's tenor.

But he said: Son, I must goin', I've got rainbows to paint
He said: Son, I must goin', I've got rainbows to paint

There was brief, spontaneous applause. The crowd loved it! The young guy was really good! He had that same honest 'take-it-or-leave-it, this-is-what-I-believe' manner as Sonny Jacobs. Joel Reed believed in every word of this song!

He had another verse to sing. Joel told them now, the weary traveler's story.

I had come to the chapel
Walkin' through a pourin' rain
My heart was filled with sorrow
I had come to ease the pain…

It was time for the chorus again, slightly different this time. Sonny's eyes willed Joel to pour out what was in his heart—and he did.

I didn't believe in angels, but I know my life was changed
By a man with an old guitar, I'll never be the same

And then the harmony again. The two men's voices dissolved into one; they were brothers…No, they were two passionate comrades sharing a wonderful story with a thousand of their closest friends.

When he said: Son, I must goin', I've got rainbows to paint
He said: Son, I must goin', I've got rainbows to paint

Their 1,000 friends showed their appreciation! The ovation was thunderous and it went on and on and on…

Sonny reached over to clasp Joel's hand. "Thank you, friend," Sonny said into the microphone. "Thank you for believing in my songs!"

Epilogue

Stan Hamilton's recovery from pancreatic cancer was miraculous! Most of his medical expenses were covered by the school's health insurance but 'patient responsibility' payments and personal expenses were astronomical. Joel Reed, the hot new Gospel and crossover-Country singer, performed a benefit concert at Oak Ridge's Bissell Park.

Reed sang all original songs, copyrighted by none other than the city's own Jenny Jacobs. For his final number, Joel performed a dedication for Stan written by Sonny Jacobs, "Tell Her There's An Angel Standing By." The benefit event raised $23,000.00 dollars for the Hamilton Family.

****

In August of 2005 Sonny Jacobs asked to be dropped from the ORPS disability register and to be re-evaluated by Tracy L. Greene, EDD.

Due to his ongoing health problems, he was unable to return to the classroom. Based upon Dr. Greene's re-evaluation, however, Coach Jacobs was allowed to serve as a volunteer assistant for the Wildcat Baseball team. The varsity baseball team was runner-up in the 2006 District tournament. Eric Barclay was named MVP of the team and earned a full scholarship to Tusculum College.

****

Custom Sound remained Sonny and Jenny's recording studio of

choice. Jerry Hinkle moved his exterminator business to a nearby vacant warehouse and turned the management over to Rose's brother-in-law, Hugh Longstone. Jerry's filmmaking crew converted his old storefront into a full-blown video production lot—the demand for Joel Reed's videos was nearly as great as for his CDs.

****

Joel Reed's 'Believers' Tour landed him the CMA Newcomer of the Year award for 2006. His collaboration with Toni Clarkston on "I Don't Want To Do This Anymore" was awarded CMA Song of the Year.

There were Dove awards, too. Jenny Jacobs was nominated in the Songwriter category for both "Angel With The Light In His Eyes" and "Bev's Song"; Joel Reed was nominated for and won the Inspirational Album of the Year Award for his CD, "Jenny's Heart."

****

Stan Hamilton and Sonny Jacobs are still in remission from cancer.

Printed in the United States
82382LV00003B/147